THE ABILENE KID: DEAD MAN'S HAND

THE ABILENE KID: DEAD MAN'S HAND

THE ABILENE KID
BOOK 1

JOHN V. MADORMO

WISE WOLF
BOOKS

WISE WOLF BOOKS
An Imprint of Wolfpack Publishing
wisewolfbooks.com
1707 E. Diana Street
Tampa, FL 33610

Paperback ISBN 978-1-965596-23-4
eBook ISBN 978-1-965596-22-7
LCCN 2025935048

To the memory of legendary lawman
James Butler "Wild Bill" Hickok
US Marshal of Abilene, Kansas in the 1870s
Upon whose life this story is loosely based.

THE ABILENE KID: DEAD MAN'S HAND

CHAPTER 1

MR. MARKUS SAT BACK IN HIS CHAIR AND SCRATCHED HIS head. "What are we going to do with you, Dominick?"

I had a feeling I knew what was coming, but I decided to play dumb. Mr. Markus and I had played this little game, but I didn't mind. He was a nice enough fellow. He had been teaching at Daniel Burnham Middle School on the northwest side of Chicago for three years now. I still remember when I first walked into his classroom. I had a huge smile on my face. This was the teacher I had been hoping for. I had heard really good things about him from other kids. And, so, now as I stood next to his desk on the last day of sixth grade, I was hoping the year would end just as it had begun. But that wasn't to be.

"Dominick, you were supposed to write an essay on *The Most Influential Person in Your Life*. Some of the other kids in class wrote about a parent or a relative or a teacher or a coach or a counselor. But you wrote about '*Lone Wolf*' *Malone*."

"Is there a problem with that?" I asked.

"Who the heck is *Lone Wolf Malone,* and how could he possibly be the most influential person in your life?"

I couldn't believe what I was hearing. Did Mr. Markus have no appreciation for one of the greatest lawmen of the Old West? Did he not realize that Lone Wolf had tamed frontier towns wherever he went? Did he not see that Amos *Lone Wolf* Malone had made it safe for widows and orphans to walk the streets at night? The man distinguished himself as a member of the Union army during the Civil War. Then went on to become the sheriff of Abilene, Kansas, from 1866 to 1888—longer than any other frontier lawman. The man was a legend.

"Mr. Markus, Amos *Lone Wolf* Malone is my personal hero. He's like my mentor. I can recite dozens of times when Lone Wolf made life safer for every man, woman, and child alive."

"I just don't get it," he said. "We're talking about a cowboy."

I refused to get angry with him. I counted to ten in my head. How could this man be so blind? Why couldn't he see that Lone Wolf was a hero—an American hero?

"Lone Wolf Malone *is* the most influential person in my life," I said. "He taught me the difference between right and wrong. He taught me the meaning of responsibility. He taught me patience and compassion. How could I pick anyone else?"

Mr. Markus sighed. "Let's try this. What if I asked you to write about the *second* most influential person in your life? Who would that be?"

I placed my finger on my lips. I thought for a moment. "I would have to say Marshall Joe '*Wild Hog*' Pittman."

He rolled his eyes. "Another Old West reference?"

"Marshall of Cheyenne, Wyoming in the 1870s."

"Okay, how about the *third* most influential?"

I needed to think about that one for a bit. A few seconds later, I had my answer. "It's gotta be Sheriff Chester '*Night Rider*' Hutchinson."

"And he was...?"

"He patrolled the streets of Amarillo, Texas from 1880 to 1887."

Mr. Markus wrung his hands. "Dominick Dalesandro, why do you have this absurd fascination with the Old West?"

Absurd? I couldn't believe what I was hearing. Mr. Markus was a teacher—a man of learning. Why couldn't he appreciate one of the most interesting and exciting periods of American history? I would need to set him straight.

"Sir, I've read countless books on the taming of the Old West. Before there were sheriffs and marshals and deputies, the territory was lawless. These selfless individuals put their own lives on the line so that decent, hard-working Americans could live in peace. How can we not admire each one of them?"

Mr. Marcus shook his head. "We're not getting anywhere, I'm afraid." He handed me my essay.

I glanced at it—a C+. The man had given me a C+. Just because he had never pretended to be a cowboy when he was a kid, he took it out on me. I bit my lip and walked to the door.

"Dominick, I can only hope your seventh-grade teacher will be able to get through to you. Have a good summer."

Yeah, and I hope my new seventh-grade teacher will be a little more open-minded. I walked into the hallway and spotted my best bud, Will Hansen, waiting for me at my locker.

"So, what was that all about?" he said.

"Mr. Marcus had a problem with *my most influential person*."

"Who'd you pick?"

"Amos *Lone Wolf* Malone."

He laughed. "Dom, you're too much."

"What is that supposed to mean?"

"The cowboy thing. The Wild West business. Dude, you gotta let it go."

"Can I help it if I'm interested in those things?"

"Interested?!" he said. "More like obsessed."

I rolled my eyes. I opened my locker and started shoveling everything into a pillowcase my mom had given me. When it appeared that I had packed up everything, I started to close the locker when Will stopped me.

"Don't forget *that*," he said, pointing.

Will was referring to a long magnet stuck to the inside of the locker door that I used to hold up my class schedule.

"Thanks," I said. I slid the magnet into my pocket. I slammed the locker shut and sighed. "Will, I just can't help myself. You're right. I am obsessed with the Wild West. It's all I think about. It's all I watch on TV. It's all I read. It's all I search on the internet. I feel like I was born a hundred and fifty years too late. I belong in the Old West."

"Oh, really?" He smiled. "The Old West, huh? Okay, here's what you're looking at." He counted them off on each finger. "No cell phones. No internet. No electricity. No air conditioning. No cars. And the big one—no indoor plumbing."

"Yeah, okay, I get that. But if we all lived in the Old

West, we wouldn't know what we were missing. None of that stuff had been invented yet."

"All I'm saying is that it was a pretty tough life back then. And if you had the chance, I don't see you trading places with anyone who lives in a wooden shack with a dirt floor and no heat."

"Are you kidding?!" I said. "I'd trade in a heartbeat."

"You say that now, but when it comes right down to it, you'd never choose that life, and we both know it."

"Will, you're my best friend. I don't want to argue with you. Let's put this discussion on hold and return to it at a later date."

"Whatever. But you'll never change. On the other hand, a healthy interest in the past isn't a bad thing. Take me, I'm fascinated with the battles of World War II, but at least that's something you'd find in history books. Who has ever heard of Amos *Lone Wolf* Malone? No one."

I had to admit—today had actually been a pretty typical day. I had argued with my teacher and with my best friend. And it always seemed to be about my interest —make that my passion—or rather my obsession, I guess —for the Old West. When I tell people I would love to have lived back then, most of them think I'm a little crazy. And they always said the same things. *Who in his right mind would ever give up the conveniences of today to live on hot, dusty prairies back in the 1800s?*

I would. But apparently, I was the only person who would. Give me a ten-gallon hat, a pair of boots, some spurs, chaps, a bedroll, and a horse, and I was a happy camper. Why couldn't anyone else see how exciting life was back then? I was getting tired of defending my position. I would just have to accept the fact that I was different than most people. There, I said it. That wasn't too painful. I assumed there weren't too many other twelve-year-olds who thought like me. And that was perfectly fine. I really didn't mind being the odd man out.

Will and I walked together for a while until we split off and each headed home. When I got there, I found my mom in the kitchen baking bread. To me, this was a normal thing. But apparently very few people still baked their own bread these days. If they wanted Italian bread, they'd just go to the supermarket or to a bakery. Not in our house. My mom grew up in a home where the aroma of fresh baked bread was commonplace. And my dad was lucky she did. He refused to eat store-bought bread. I used to beg my mom to buy a loaf of American bread from the supermarket. I wore her down one day and she bought some. It was the first time and the last time she did. When she set it out at the dinner table, my dad grabbed a piece of it and rolled it into a ball.

"Do you expect me to eat this?" he said. "It's dough!"

"Sorry, Dominick," my mom said. "I told you."

"Did you put your mother up to this?" he said to me.

"Dad, at school, everyone brings sandwiches made from this kind of bread. They don't complain. They like it just fine."

"They don't know what they're missing," he said. "You just give them a piece of Italian bread with the hard crust." He laughed. "They'll never buy that store-bought garbage again."

And so, as I passed through the kitchen on my way into the living room and upstairs to my room, I snatched a piece of warm homemade bread off the counter and stuffed it into my mouth. As I was chewing, I started thinking about the Old West again. I suddenly realized that a lot of ranchers and farmers who lived back in the

1800s lived on homemade bread. I was actually getting a taste of frontier living without knowing it. I decided at that very moment never to complain about my mom's homemade Italian bread for as long as I lived. She was preparing me for life in the Wild West if I ever somehow made it back there.

I removed the books, notebooks, and school supplies from the pillowcase and tossed them in my closet. I had three months before I'd have to worry about them again.

"Dominick?"

I heard my mom's voice at the stairs.

"Yeah."

"Don't forget you have a haircut at three o'clock. You should be leaving right now."

"Okay." I had completely forgotten. I ran downstairs, flew out the back door, and into the garage. I hopped on my bike and was on my way. It would take me no more than ten minutes to get there. A little while later, I pulled up in front of Tony's Hair Salon and Spa on Grand Avenue. Not long ago, the name of the shop was Tony the Barber. He had changed the name with the hopes of attracting new business—a younger clientele perhaps—but every time I was there, I would always see the same old men sitting around shooting the breeze.

When I walked in, I waved to Tony and took a seat. Tony was a likable sort. He was nearing eighty but still going strong. He had cut my dad's hair since he was a boy, so he naturally became my barber. Even at his advanced age, he was still pretty sharp. There appeared to be one more person in front of me. I decided to look for something to read to kill the time. I began searching for one particular book. I went from rack to rack looking for it. Not here. Not there. Where the heck was it?

"What are you looking for, Dominick?" Tony asked.

"You know, that one book I always read."

Tony scratched the top of his head. "Oh, that one. It's on that little table against the wall. It's on the bottom under all the others. You're the only one who ever reads it."

"Thanks." I scooted over, dug under a bunch of coffee table books, and finally found it. Yes! *Famous Lawmen of the Old West* by Bill O'Keefe. I immediately went to page 178. And there he was—Amos *Lone Wolf* Malone. I couldn't get enough of this guy. I couldn't ever remember reading one bad thing about him. Everyone seemed to love Sheriff Malone. He cleaned up towns wherever he went. His last assignment was sheriff of Abilene, Kansas. He ran the town for nearly twenty-two years...before his untimely death at the age of fifty-nine.

Sheriff Malone liked to wind down each day with a friendly game of poker at the Ranchview Saloon. One particular night a man by the name of Moses Tanahill, who had been drinking heavily, sat down at the table. He proceeded to lose large amounts of money, while the sheriff was on a winning streak. This didn't sit well with the gambler. Sheriff Malone suggested the man quit playing to cut his losses. He even offered him money for breakfast the next day. The gambler grudgingly accepted his charity. The next night the sheriff walked into the saloon to play cards. Lone Wolf always liked to sit with his back to the wall so he could see whoever might be entering the saloon. But that night the only seat open was a chair facing away from the door. He asked a couple of players to switch seats with him, but both refused. He reluctantly sat down at the open seat. Moments later, without warning, Tanahill rushed in and shot Sheriff Malone. It was the last game of poker he ever played.

I can't tell you how many times I've read that passage. And every time, I find myself feeling just awful. It just wasn't fair. The town—for that matter, the territory—lost one of the best men to have ever roamed the plains of Kansas. I wished I could have been there to have warned the sheriff. Every time I start daydreaming about that night, I see myself sitting at a table near the action, spotting the reckless gunman, and yelling out to Sheriff Malone. But there was no one there to warn him. Over time, the cards the sheriff was holding that night became known as the *Dead Man's Hand*—two aces and two eights.

Sheriff Amos *Lone Wolf* Malone was a legend in the Kansas territory. I can't tell you how many times he broke up gunfights before they led to someone's death. He avoided using a gun whenever possible. Half the time he walked the streets of Abilene without carrying one. He believed that most people could be set on a straight and narrow path with mercy and compassion. I can't tell you how many would-be criminals were saved by this kind and noble sheriff. And Lone Wolf was a friend to many of the Native American tribes in Kansas. He even spoke Arapaho, Cheyenne, Kiowa, and Pawnee. When others wanted to strip the lands away from these tribes and banish them to a reservation, it was Amos Malone who defended these early Americans. He took the position that these tribes were the rightful owners of the lands they settled, and claim jumpers had no business running them off. As you might guess, this was not a very popular position in those days.

"Dominick?" Tony said. "It's your turn. You can bring the book with you if you like."

Startled, I jumped up and hopped into Tony's chair. "Sorry, I was caught up in something."

"I could tell," he said. "So, why don't you tell me all about Lone Wolf Malone. I know you're dying to."

"I can't believe you remembered his name."

Tony laughed. "For as many times as you've told me about that sheriff, how could I forget?"

For the next half hour, I told Tony about the greatest lawman in the history of the Old West. Even though he had heard this story countless times, he pretended like it was the first time.

"You know," he said, "last week the wife and I were in here cleaning out old magazines and books. She pulled out the one you're holding and asked me if we should get rid of it."

"Perish the thought," I said.

"I told her that a very special client, one Dominick Dalesandro, would be heartbroken if we were to get rid of that book."

"Apparently, she took your advice," I said.

"She did, but it took me a little while to convince her."

"Thanks, Tony. I don't know what I'd have done if you had gotten rid of it."

"Don't worry," he said. "As long as you're a customer, *Famous Lawmen of the Old West* will always be in my collection of reading material."

That was what I loved about Tony. He was the best.

CHAPTER 2

THE NEXT MORNING, I SLEPT IN. IT WAS THE FIRST OFFICIAL day of summer vacation. No more seven a.m. alarm. I didn't wake up until eight thirty, and it felt great. I rose leisurely and dressed. Just to make sure no one had invaded my inner sanctum, I crouched down and slid out the foot locker I kept hidden under my bed. It housed all of my prized possessions. I fingered the combination carefully—7, 11, 18, 88. It was an easy set of numbers to remember—the day that Lone Wolf Malone had died— July 11, 1888.

When I flipped open the locker, I was staring at some of my prized possessions—a pair of square-toe Western cowboy boots, a classic white cattleman cowboy hat, a red-and-white bandanna, a pair of roping spurs with floral engraving, a longhorn belt buckle, a cowboy bolo tie with cowhide rope, imitation leather saddlebags, and a set of suede cowboy chaps. The boots, the belt buckle, and the hat were exact replicas of those worn by Amos Malone. I had been saving up my allowance for years in order to buy these things. I never really used them outside of my own bedroom though. Every so often when no one was home, I would dress up in my cowboy gear and pretend I was facing an outlaw at sundown on Main Street, playing poker at the nearby gambling hall, or charming a little lady at the local saloon.

I knew that a lot of my friends daydreamed about hitting the game-winning grand slam in the bottom of the ninth, throwing a touchdown pass as the game was about to end, hitting a three-pointer at the buzzer, scoring a goal on a fifty-foot slap shot in overtime, etc. So, what's the difference between what they do and what I do. Why then did my passion seem so weird to everyone else? For fear of being teased, I hadn't told any of my friends about the contents of my foot locker—all my friends except Will, that is. He doesn't get it, but he at least never gives me a hard time about it. That was how it was with a best friend. It was someone who you could share your deep, dark secrets with. I was glad I had someone I could talk to about this stuff.

"Hey, what is that?"

I slammed the foot locker shut. My nosy older sister had invaded my privacy.

"What's in there?" she said. "Is that a hat?"

"It isn't anything. And it's none of your business," I said. "Get out! Right now!" I slid the locker under my bed.

"Get out! Right now!" she said, mimicking me. "I have a good mind to tell Mom what you're hiding under there."

"Go ahead and tell her. See if I care." I pointed to the door. "Out! And don't step into this room ever again."

She turned, flicked her hair, and exited. "You're such a loser."

I waited until I was sure she was gone. Phew! That was a close one. My sister, Angie, was the last—and I mean the last—person in the world I would ever want to know what I had in that case. She'd never let me hear the end of it.

I walked over and closed the door. I couldn't remember how many times I had asked my parents if I could get a lock on my bedroom door. My dad would always say, "One of these days I'll get around to it," but he never had. I might just take the matter into my own hands someday. I decided I needed to be more careful with my cowboy stuff with my sister in the room across the hall. She was bound to stick her head in at any time. And since she was the biggest busybody around, I would really need to protect my privacy. My sister had nothing else to do with her time. She spent the entire day on her cell phone gabbing with her friends. They would gossip the entire time. I guessed that was what you did when you were in high school, but it sure seemed like a complete waste of time to me.

I ran downstairs, grabbed a quick breakfast, and was out the door. I jumped on my bike and headed to my personal sanctuary—the local library. Most days after school, I would spend time there. Sometimes I would do homework, but most of the time I would read Old West books. I had read every book in our public library that had any mention of Amos *Lone Wolf* Malone in it. And in doing so, I learned a ton about all the other Wild West lawmen as well.

When I walked in the front door, I spotted Mrs. West-phal sitting at the circulation desk.

"Good morning, Dominick," she said.

"Have you gotten in any new Old West books?" I asked.

She shook her head. "You ask me that every day. And every day, my answer is *no*."

"How come you don't stock more of those books?"

"Well, here's the problem. As fascinating as you may find that topic, there just aren't many authors writing about the Wild West anymore. Every so often, a book will pop up, but it's very rare."

"Oh, well, I guess I'll just have to re-read some of my old favorites." I turned to leave but immediately stopped. "I do have one more question."

"Fire away," she said.

"The year was 1869. The location was Stillwater, Oklahoma. Ike Dirksen was being held on suspicion of bank robbery. Name the sheriff who single-handedly held off the Dirksen Gang when they tried to break him out of jail."

"Dominick, you're going to have to do better than that," she said. "The answer is Sheriff Lucius Bolton."

"Darn!" I sighed and composed myself. "Okay, your turn."

"Okay, let me think." She paused momentarily. "All right, I have one. The year was 1875. Three outlaws held up the Western Plains Stagecoach on its way from Midland, Texas to Carlsbad, New Mexico. They got away with twenty-two thousand dollars in government bonds. Name the sheriff who tracked them down and brought them to justice—*and* who recovered all of the stolen bonds."

I smiled.

"Seems like you might be getting a little overconfident?" Mrs. Westphal said.

I took my time. I wanted her to know that she couldn't stump me that easily. "Sounds like Sheriff John Jay Wrightwood to me."

She grinned. "Nicely done."

"Okay, my turn again. The year was..."

Mrs. Westphal held up her hand. "Dominick, I'd like nothing better than to play Old West trivia with you, but I really have to get back to work. I'm sorry."

"Oh, that's okay. I'll save it for tomorrow."

"You do that," she said. "I'll have one for you too."

"Great. See you later." I always loved quizzing Mrs. Westphal. She was the only other person I knew who could hold her own when it came to Wild West history. No one else seemed to care about the topic as much as she or I did. I'll tell you why Mrs. Westphal is so well-informed. In her younger days, she was a high school history teacher. Her specialty was the American frontier from 1850 to 1900. That was what she did her thesis on in grad school. So, naturally, she would know all about famous lawmen and outlaws of the Old West.

I walked through the main part of the library to a stairwell on the far end of the building. I went downstairs to the lower level. I loved it down there. The air conditioning really cranked. It was like an icebox, but I was perfectly fine with that. It was also a little darker. The lighting created a cozier setting. Instead of the desks and tables they had upstairs, the lower level was furnished with bright-colored beanbag chairs. You could really get comfortable in one of those. And it just so happened that all of the library's holdings on the Old West happened to be stored down there.

I hopped up on a stool and began checking the top shelf of a long rack of books. Every title I came across, I had already read. I kept hoping I might find a book that I had overlooked in the past, or one that had snuck by Mrs. Westphal. But no such luck. It was just all the old standards. I decided to grab the biggest one on the shelf—*An*

Encyclopedia of the Old West. I was determined to get from A to Z before the end of summer vacation. This book unfortunately was one of those reference books that you weren't allowed to check out. I'd have to start it and finish it in the library.

I stepped down and found a comfy beanbag chair. I flipped open the book that was weighing me down and got to work. I had only managed to read about an *abra*, an *acequia*, and an *acorn calf* when I heard someone coming down the stairs.

"I knew I'd find you here." It was Will.

"What are you doing here?" I said.

"I called your house, but your mom wasn't sure where you were. This is the first place I tried, and as usual, I was right."

Will was the only person other than Mrs. Westphal who seemed to understand my passion for the Old West. Based on the negative reactions from some of the other kids at school, I kept this topic fairly low key. Fortunately, Will and Mrs. Westphal weren't judgy about it. Will was somewhat familiar with my routine. He knew that I spent most afternoons at the library, and he knew that most of the time, I wasn't doing homework. He walked over and peeked at the book I was reading.

"Some *heavy* reading, huh?"

I held up the book as best I could. It had to have weighed a ton. "No kidding. You know, I think I've read every single book down here."

"Hey, it's a beautiful day, Dominick. Let's go have a little fun."

"What did you have in mind?"

"I passed by that construction site where the new apartment building's going up. There weren't any workmen around. I thought we might do a little exploring."

"Exploring?"

He smiled. "Allies vs. Axis powers."

I smiled. "You mean us versus the Nazis again." I think the reason Will didn't bug me much about my obsession with the Wild West was because he had a passion of his own—World War II. A construction site was the perfect location to pretend we were looking for survivors in a bombed-out building in Europe in 1943.

"As long as I don't have to be Heinrich Himmler again," I said.

"Okay, we'll both be allies this time. I'll be a first lieutenant under General Patton, and you can be a downed British airman. How's that sound?"

"I got shot down? Again? Doesn't say much for my flying skills."

He sat down. "All right, you were in a major dogfight with a squadron of German Messerschmitt ME 210s. You managed to shoot down a half dozen of them before your plane took a fatal hit to the engine compartment. Is that better?"

"What am I flying?"

Will thought to himself. "Let's see. Okay. You were in a single-seat Hawker Hurricane."

"Ooh, I like the sound of that." As much as I just wanted to be left alone to read about the Old West, I had to admit that I did have a tiny bit of interest in pretending to be a participant in WWII. If it was anyone other than Will, I would probably have declined. But since he had sat through my endless rambling about cowboys and such over the years, I figured I kind of owed it to him to give in to one of his requests. I closed up the Old West encyclopedia, hopped up on the cart, and slid it back onto the shelf.

The construction site was about a ten-minute walk from the library. When we arrived, we found a chain-link fence surrounding the property, and a red-and-white sign as big as day which read: *NO TRESPASSING. This area is a restricted construction site. Anyone found trespassing on this property shall upon conviction be guilty of a FELONY.* Apparently, we weren't welcome.

Will noticed me reading the sign. "Aw, don't pay any attention to that. They just put that up there to scare people. Nothing'll happen even if we do get caught."

"I've never been arrested before," I said.

"Don't think of it as if you were a convict or something. Just pretend you're a prisoner of war. It sounds more honorable."

I looked at the barbed wire on top of the chain-link fence. "We'll never get over that," I said.

"Who said anything about going *over*."

"Huh?"

"C'mon."

I followed Will to the back of the construction site where there was a gate.

"All you gotta do is suck in your stomach," he said. He moved the gate forward which created an opening about six inches wide. He stuck his head through first, then his shoulder, then his hips. A moment later, he was on the other side. "Voilà."

I took his lead, sucked in my gut, and did my best to squeeze through. I had managed to get the top half of my body through the opening, but I had to take off my belt to get the bottom half through. Seconds later, I was in.

"See," he said. "No barbed wire."

"If we get caught, it'll be tough to make a hasty exit."

"You worry too much. C'mon."

The apartment building was about halfway done. The structure was completely framed out. There was one set of stairs connecting the first floor to the second floor but no way to access the third floor. We climbed in and began our adventure.

"Okay, now, you lie down right there," he said. "Here's the scene: I walk in and find you unconscious. I get you to your feet and then we make our way through the burned-out rubble looking for civilians."

I shrugged. Whatever. I lay down and closed my eyes.

"What do we have here?" Will said. "Looks like a Brit." He leaned over me. "He's still alive." He looked up. "There's his parachute." He crouched down next to me. "Hey, mate, wake up." He shook me.

I slowly opened my eyes. "Where am I?"

"We're about forty miles north of Marseille."

"Are you a Yankee?" I asked.

He smiled. "Born and bred in Scranton, Pennsylvania." He grabbed my arm. "Let's get you on your feet."

I stood up and looked around. "Do you suppose there are any survivors?"

"It doesn't look good. Let's check."

We climbed up the stairs onto the second floor and walked around.

"I'm afraid they're all goners," Will said. "Like they say, 'War is hell.'"

We looked down to the street and saw a yellow truck pull up in front of the site. Two men in hard hats stepped out.

"Hit the floor!" Will said.

We dropped onto our stomachs.

"Do you think they saw us?" I asked.

"I don't think so. Let's stay here for a minute."

But by then it was too late.

"Hey, you kids, get out of there right now or we're calling the cops!"

We scrambled to our feet, jumped down to the first-floor landing, and headed for the back gate. Will got there first. He quickly slithered through the opening. We could hear the men's voices. They were getting louder.

"Hurry, Dom."

I inhaled and tried to squeeze through. I had managed to get the majority of my body out but a loop on one of my shoelaces got caught on a piece of metal.

"Will, help!" We could hear footsteps.

Will tried to get me free but only managed to make it worse. "It's really stuck," he said.

"You kids are in big trouble!" a voice called out.

"Sorry, dude," Will said. "This is the only way." He grabbed at my heel and slid my foot out of the shoe.

"Let's get outta here!" he said.

"I can't leave my shoe here."

"It's either that or a stretch in Leavenworth," he said. "Take your pick." Will flew out of the construction site and down the street.

I looked back and shook my head. How was I ever going to explain to my parents why I was only wearing one shoe? I'd have to come up with something really good, and hope they'd buy it.

CHAPTER 3

WHEN I WALKED INTO THE KITCHEN FOR BREAKFAST THE next morning, my mom immediately caught sight of my footwear.

"Why are you wearing those old running shoes? They have holes in the bottoms. You should be wearing your new pair."

That, however, was the problem—only one shoe left from the new pair. Late yesterday afternoon, Will and I made a return visit to the construction site with the hopes of retrieving my ill-fated shoe. We needed to make sure the two construction workers who had seen us earlier in the day weren't around. When we got there, it was relatively quiet. We looked for our uninvited guests, but they were nowhere in sight. We tiptoed up to the back gate and looked for my missing shoe. We must have looked for a good half hour. It had completely disappeared. Those construction workers must have had a good old time anni-hilating the property of the kid who had given them the slip. My shoe had probably been shredded into a million pieces by now. I knew I'd never find it.

So, that was why I was wearing my shoes with holes in the bottoms at breakfast. I hadn't really thought my mom would pick up on the old shoes so quickly. I expected to have a couple of days to come up with a really imaginative story of how I had lost my shoe. The pressure was on. Did I have the necessary creative juices to think up a believable story? I pressed my fingers against my temples. I had to get things percolating up there. And I had to do so before my dad sat down at the table. He was skeptical of everything and everybody. Since it was a Saturday, my dad was available to join us for breakfast. He appeared a moment later.

"What did I just hear you talking about with your mother? Something about shoes?"

Oh, no. This was just great. I needed to come up with a real doozy. "I just decided to wear the old ones. I didn't want to put any more miles on the new pair. That way they'll last longer." There—I had done it. The explanation seemed perfectly logical to me. I was only hoping they would buy it.

"Dominick, the problem is that those old shoes aren't good for your feet," my mom said. "You could step on something, and it could go right into your foot."

"Then you'll need a tetanus shot," my dad said. "And I don't think you want that."

How do I come back from that? "I'll be careful where I step. Don't worry." I tried to seem nonchalant about it, but I had a bad feeling this conversation wasn't over.

My mom spooned some scrambled eggs onto my plate and then my dad's. She set the frying pan back on the stove, grabbed a towel, and wiped off her hands.

"I don't want any arguments," she said. "I'm going to

get those new shoes for you right now." She was halfway out of the kitchen when I stopped her.

"Mom, please don't do that."

"Why?" she said.

"Well...there's a problem."

"What kind of problem?" my dad said.

This was the best I could come up with. "You see, Will and I were walking home from the library yesterday when we decided to take a shortcut home. It was an area we weren't familiar with. And then, all of the sudden, this vicious dog comes flying out from between two houses and runs right at us. Let me tell you—we took off. But the dog eventually caught up to us. He latched onto my right shoe and began gnawing on it. I pulled and pulled to try to break free, but nothing worked. The only thing I could think of doing was to just let him have the shoe. So, I did. We started running again and fortunately he didn't follow us. I don't know what ever happened to the shoe. It's probably all chewed up by now. And that's why I'm wearing my old running shoes."

My dad folded his arms and looked at me skeptically.

My mom was beside herself. "Well, you should have told someone, Dominick. We need to call the police and report that animal. There's a leash law in this town. That dog should be locked up. And his owner owes us a brand new pair of shoes."

"That's okay," I said. "I don't want to get anyone in trouble."

"Sure, it's okay with you because you didn't have to pay for them," my dad said.

"If you want *me* to replace them," I said. "I'm happy to do that. Of course, I'll need about six month's advance on my allowance."

"Money is not the issue," my mom said.

"What?" my dad replied. "Of course it is!"

I wolfed down the scrambled eggs. I needed to vacate the premises as quickly as possible. This had suddenly turned into a money discussion which always turned into a money argument.

"I gotta go. But we can continue this discussion at a later date. I'm headed to the library. See you later." I shot out the back door before either of them could react. I could hear them arguing right through the closed door. I lifted each foot to see how bad the holes were on the old shoes. Ooh, not very good. I would need to be careful. Couldn't step on any rusty nails.

I decided to take a new route to the library so if I ever needed to, I'd be able to identify the street where this imaginary dog had come from. On the way, I didn't see anything unusual. I was actually hoping to find a few dogs who might be good candidates if I ever needed to retell my story.

When I got to the library, I walked right up to Mrs. Westphal. She was on the phone. As soon as she hung up, I struck.

"The year was 1866. The Dixon Brothers had just robbed their third bank in a month in the Arizona territory. Their next stop was Tombstone. But the law there was waiting for them. Name the marshal who disguised himself as a bank teller and managed to bring all four of the Dixon Brothers to justice without firing a shot."

Mrs. Westphal tilted her head and smiled. "Let me see now. You must be referring to Marshal Elijah Gladstone."

"Oh, man," I said. "I thought for sure I'd stump you with that one."

"You almost did," she said.

"Do you have one for me?"

"I certainly do. It was 1879 in the Dakota territory. Name the lawman who single-handedly rounded up a cattle-rustling ring, the largest to date."

I thought to myself for a minute. I knew this one. It was on the tip of my tongue.

"Have I stumped you?" she said.

"I need a few more seconds."

She nodded.

"Okay...it wasn't...no, that's not it. Wait a minute, I got it. Sheriff Stanhouse *No Neck* Gridley."

Mrs. Westphal laughed. "I don't think you've ever missed any of my questions."

"I'd be disappointed in myself if I ever did. It would be really depressing."

"Oh, it wouldn't be that bad, Dominick."

"Oh, yes it would. I pride myself on being an expert on lawmen of the Old West."

She looked around. She motioned for me to follow her. "Come with me. There's something I want to show you." She waved to another library employee a couple of desks over. "Sheila, can you watch my phone for a minute?"

I followed Mrs. Westphal to one of the offices. She sat down at a desk and opened a drawer. She pulled out a dusty, dirty old book.

"Do you know what this is?" she asked.

I shook my head.

She turned it so I could read the title.

"Oh my gosh! Where did you find this?"

"We were cleaning out some of the closets where we store old books. When I spotted this one, I grabbed it. I knew you had to see it."

On the front cover were the words, *The Man Who Tamed the Wild West. The Unauthorized Biography of Amos "Lone Wolf" Malone* by Don Kent.

"I've never seen this book before," I said.

"Well, this one is unlike any of other books you've read here at the library." She opened the book to the second page. "Dominick, this book is a first edition. It's very rare. It was published in 1895."

I had to see this book. I had to read it. Would Mrs. Westphal let me? I needed to find out.

"Is this something I'd be able to read?"

"All of our first editions are locked up in the library vault. None of them are on the shelves."

"Is that where this one is headed?" I asked. I was afraid to hear her answer.

"By all rights, I should march this book directly to the vault. But..." She looked around. "I think it might be okay for you to take a look at it."

"Really?"

She reached for a plastic bag with the library logo on it. She slid the book into the bag and handed it to me.

"You can't take it out of the building. You can only read it while you're here. Understood?"

"Understood."

"I assume you're headed to your favorite spot," Mrs. Westphal said.

"Oh, you know about that, huh?"

She smiled. "I like going down to the lower level myself. Now make sure you bring the book back to me when you leave. I'll hold it in my desk until you're done reading it."

"I really appreciate this," I said.

"I know you do. Now go downstairs and get cracking."

"Thanks again." I took off like a dart in the direction of the stairwell. I ran down the stairs and looked around. I didn't want anyone to see what I was holding. And I sure didn't want to see Mrs. Westphal get into any trouble. I looked behind all of the bookcases to make sure I was alone. Then I found the most comfortable beanbag chair and settled in. I glanced at my hands and realized I was shaking. I couldn't believe I had never come across this treasure. I was certain I had read everything ever published on Amos Malone. It looked like I was wrong.

I scanned the room one last time for any sign of intruders. Once I was sure I was alone, I slid the book out of the plastic bag and just stared at it—*The Man Who Tamed the Wild West. The Unauthorized Biography of Amos "Lone Wolf" Malone.* I was almost afraid to open it. I took a deep breath and slowly lifted the cover. I noticed a thick coating of dust on the first page. I carefully blew it off, and was about to proceed when I realized that the dust particles seemed to be hovering just overhead. It was as if they refused to float to the ground. They began to swirl and glitter. What was happening? I held the book at arm's length. The cloud of dust was growing in size. The particles began to sparkle. What the heck was going on?

Then the dust particles began to take shape...the shape of a figure...a man...in a vest...in boots...and a cowboy hat. As the remaining particles trickled to the floor, I could hardly believe my eyes. It was as if the figure had stepped right out of an 1880s book...in fact, he had!

"Sh...Sh...Sheriff Malone?!"

The figure brushed the dust from his vest. "Who were you expecting? Billy the Kid?"

It was Sheriff Amos *Lone Wolf* Malone. In the flesh. His face matched every picture I had ever seen of him. It was the same belt buckle. The same square-toe boots. The same white cowboy hat. What was happening? This was crazy. I wanted to get out of there as quickly as possible, but my legs wouldn't move. It was like one of those dreams where you're being chased and you start running —but you're running in slow motion. I couldn't lift myself off the beanbag chair. It was as if I was glued to it. And it had something to do with this image hovering over me. Where had this guy come from?

"Is it really you?"

Dust particles filled the room as the sheriff removed his hat and banged it on the side of his leg.

"It's me, little buddy, relax."

"But how...I mean...how did you?"

Sheriff Malone stretched his arms and groaned. "Do you have any idea how long I been cooped up in there?"

"Are...are you real?"

"Depends on what you mean by real." He pulled a cigar from his shirt pocket, bit the tip off and spit it onto the floor. "Got a light?"

"Oh, I'm afraid you can't smoke in here," I said.

Lone Wolf made a face and rolled his eyes.

"And those things are bad for you too."

"What are you talking about?! This is like eating a candy bar."

"No way. They're dangerous. You don't want to end up with lung cancer or heart disease, do you?"

Sheriff Malone looked at the stogey, shook his head, and slid it back into his pocket.

"Stand up, Dominick."

I slowly got to my feet. "You know my name?"

The sheriff chuckled. "Know your *name*? Shucks, I

know everything about you. Just like you know everything about me."

I fell back into the chair. "I don't get it."

"This isn't some chance meeting, my young friend. You were supposed to find that book."

"I was?"

Lone Wolf plopped down into one of the beanbag chairs and put his feet up on the table.

"As you can see, I ain't getting' any younger. And, to tell you the truth, I'm a little tired of duckin' flying lead." He produced a toothpick and began gnawing on it. "I'm looking for someone to take over the sheriff's office when I retire." He raised his eyebrows and smiled.

I looked around the room. He couldn't be talking about me, right? Heck, I'm just a kid. How could I possibly be expected to run the sheriff's office?

I pointed at myself. "You mean...?"

"Yeah, son, you. I can't think of anyone more qualified. You know more about me than I do."

"Soooo, how would this work?"

He grinned. "It's all very simple." He sat up and leaned forward. "You come back to the Old West with me and learn the ropes. Then we'll change the sign on the door to *Sheriff Dominick Dal—*" He stopped in mid-sentence. "Well, we'll have to get you a new name. Dominick Dalesandro will never fly back in Abilene. You'll need something short and sweet. And something with fewer vowels in it. Those cowboys can be a rough bunch. What do you say?"

This was all happening too quickly. What exactly was he asking me to do? I mean, for years, I had fantasized about living in the Old West, but I never expected it to actually happen.

"How exactly do we get to your office?"

He pointed to the door on the far wall. It read STAFF – NO ADMITTANCE.

"All we have to do is go right through that door."

"But that door's always locked."

"Not for us," he said. "Are you game?"

Was this guy nuts? How was this possible? We walk through an office door and somehow travel back a hundred-plus years? This was unreal. I needed to proceed cautiously.

"Okay, let's say I decided to join you. How would I get back if I changed my mind later on?"

Sheriff Malone seemed irritated. He stood over me. "Listen, Dom, you've been dreaming about being a cowboy and living on the prairie for as long as I can remember. You've always wanted a taste of the Wild West." He walked over to the staff door and grabbed the handle. "It's right here. Let's go."

"I...I just don't know." I knew it wasn't what he wanted to hear, but did he really expect me to just go with him and leave everything behind? Wouldn't people worry about me? And what exactly was I getting myself into?

The sheriff turned away and sighed. "Well, it looks like I misread this one." He tugged on his belt buckle and straightened his hat. "There's a youngster in Altoona, Pennsylvnia, who'll jump at this chance."

"No, wait!" I couldn't think straight. I was afraid to go with him. But if this was one of those once-in-a-lifetime opportunities, I'd never forgive myself for passing it up. He was right. This was what I had always dreamed of. I *did* want a taste of adventure. But at what price? Would it be dangerous? People got killed in the Old West. Could that happen to me? I could tell he was growing impatient. He wanted an answer—fast, but I had one more question.

"Sheriff, what about my parents, and my friends. Won't they be wondering what happened to me?"

"They'll never notice," he said.

"I don't get it."

"Once you come with me, and you're transported back to the Old West, time will stand still. No one'll miss you 'cause they won't know you're gone. And when you return, you'll end up right back here in this room at the exact minute you left. Are you in?"

I wanted to. I really did. So, why was I so wishy-washy? And then suddenly something popped into my head. Of course. Why hadn't I thought of it before? This was my chance to rewrite history. I glanced at the calendar on the wall. It read June 11th.

"Sheriff, what year is it right now in Abilene?"

"1888. What's that have to do with anything?"

The timing couldn't have been more perfect. Sheriff Amos *Lone Wolf* Malone would be shot down one month from today while playing poker in the Ranchview Saloon. If I agreed to go back with him, I could be in the saloon on that fateful night. I could stop his assailant in the act. It was my civic duty to do everything in my power to help save the greatest sheriff to ever walk the frontier plains.

"I'm waiting."

Wait a minute. Wait just one minute. What was I thinking? I didn't have to go back with him to save his life. I could just tell him not to play poker on July 11th. Yeah. That would work.

"Sheriff, there's something I need to tell you."

"What's that?"

"Well, it's kind of hard to say. It's about you and what happens to you."

Sheriff Malone threw his arms up. "Dominick, I have a feeling I know what you're about to tell me. It's something that will take place in my future, right?"

"Yeah!"

"Don't waste your breath, son. You can't tell me."

"But why?"

"We can't mess with destiny. Things happen for a reason, and we have to respect that."

"But it's a matter of life and death."

"Doesn't matter." The sheriff pulled out a pocket watch, glanced at it, and frowned. "We gotta get going, boy. I shouldn't be away from the office this long." He tapped on the face of his watch. "Time's a wastin'."

I had run out of time. The sheriff needed an answer right now. I wasn't sure why I was having such a hard time making up my mind. The answer seemed fairly obvious. Since the sheriff wouldn't let me warn him about what was going to happen in his life, I would have no other choice but to go back to Abilene with him. It was the only way to save the man's life. It appeared the decision to stay or go had been made for me. I took a deep breath.

"Okay," I said. "I'm in."

A smile appeared on the sheriff's face. "I knew I could count on you. Okay, gimme your hand."

I reached out slowly.

Sheriff Malone grabbed it. His grip was tight. "Now close your eyes and think about outlaws...and bank robbers...and cattle rustlers...and..."

I began to squirm. "What?!" Was it too late to get out?

The sheriff seemed to sense my nervousness. "Just kidding," he said with a smirk.

I sighed. I was in, and there was no going back now. Soon the dust particles reappeared just above the table. The cloud descended and seemed to surround us. It started to spin and glow and glitter. It moved to each corner of the room. Then it returned and hovered over the open book. I began to feel as though something was tugging at my feet, pulling at me, lifting me up into the air. The cloud traveled over to the door which opened by itself. We were being sucked into the open doorway. Something told me to fight it, but I couldn't. A moment later, Sheriff Amos *Lone Wolf* Malone and I were swallowed up.

CHAPTER 4

WHEN I OPENED MY EYES, I FOUND MYSELF NOT IN THE COZY corner of the library basement, but in a tunnel of some sort. It was pitch black.

"Just grab on to the back of my belt and follow me," the sheriff said.

"Where are we?" I asked.

"You'll see."

We walked about fifty yards where the tunnel came to a dead end. I could just barely make out a ladder dug into the wall.

Sheriff Malone pointed up. "This way."

I followed him up the ladder until we reached a trap door of some sort. He pushed up on it until it dislodged. He climbed up out of the tunnel. I followed him.

"Well, what do you think?" he said.

"What is this?"

"It's my office." He walked a few feet and threw open a heavy wooden door. "And here's the jail. This is it. Home sweet home."

I looked around the room. The floor was dusty. There

was a buffalo-hide rug in the middle of it. On the walls were wanted posters. There was a rifle rack hanging over a cabinet. A large, metal safe sat on the floor behind the desk. In the corner there was some sort of stove with a rusty coffee pot sitting on top. Next to the door was a hatrack. On the opposite side of the room were two crude bunks with the skinniest mattresses I had ever seen. Those couldn't be too comfortable. The Ritz, this was not.

"Well? Is it what you always imagined?"

"I...I guess. Yeah, it is." I leaned over and looked into the jail. There were four cells. And someone was sleeping in one of them. I smiled at the sheriff. "Bank robber? Cattle rustler?"

"'Fraid not. That unlucky gentleman had a little too much to drink last night. He started busting things up at the saloon."

"Will he have to go on trial?"

"Nah. He just needs to sleep it off. He will have to reimburse the saloon owner for the damages though. Then he's free to go."

"Did he put up a fight?"

Sheriff Malone shook his head. "It was an easy arrest. He could barely walk."

I noticed a six-shooter and a holster hanging on the wall. "Aren't you gonna put that on?"

"Only if I absolutely have to. And most times I don't." He studied my face. "Not as exciting as you were hoping, huh?"

"Well, I don't know. I'm sure you can't be facing down dangerous desperados every day."

"It doesn't happen too often. And I'm fine with that. I'd like to be around for a long time."

Apparently, the sheriff was expecting to live a long life,

but he had no idea what was in store for him. I had to try one more time. I had to tell him what was going to happen a month from now.

"Sheriff, there's something I'd like to discuss with you."

He sat down behind his desk and pointed to a chair on the other side.

"It has to do with your future."

He threw his head back. "Here we go again. Dominick, you can't tell me what's going to happen in the future."

"But it's really, really important."

He shook his head. "Ain't gonna happen."

"But I don't understand. Why won't you let me tell you about something bad that's going to happen?"

"Dominick, don't you see. If you try to change the future, everything that follows will be affected by it, and it might not turn out the way you hoped. You can't change history. I know it's hard for you to understand. But what the future holds is bigger than both of us. Good or bad, we just have to accept it. Promise me you won't say anything."

I didn't know what to say. If someone else knew when and how *I* was going to die, I would definitely want them to tell me. Anyone would. Why would it be wrong to change history for the better? How could saving Sheriff Malone's life be anything but good? I just didn't get it.

"Sheriff, if you really don't want me to say anything, I guess I won't. But if you ever change your mind, you gotta let me know."

"Don't worry. I won't." He sighed. "Dominick, promise me."

Why was he doing this? He was making it really hard for me to go back on my word. I had never broken a promise before. But I just didn't think that breaking this one would be a big deal. The only reason I was here was to save his life.

I took a deep breath and blew it out. "Okay, I promise."

"Good." He slapped the top of the desk. "Now we can get down to business." He got up and walked over to the stove. "Can I get you a cup of coffee?"

"No thanks. I don't drink coffee."

"You're probably better off. I have to admit—I make a really bad pot of coffee." He poured himself a cup and took a sip. "Hey, I got an idea. How about if I show you around town?"

"That'd be great," I said.

"By the way, in case we bump into someone, and I need to introduce you, have you thought about a new name to call yourself."

"Not yet, but I'll come up with something. Don't worry."

"Think about it." He walked over and opened the door. "It's time for the residents of Abilene, Kansas to meet their next sheriff. C'mon, boy."

I followed Sheriff Malone out to the sidewalk, which was actually made of wood. The boards creaked as we walked on them. The sheriff took a few steps and stopped.

"This right here is the telegraph office. You know what a telegraph is, right?"

I nodded.

"Good, less to explain." He walked a few more feet and pointed to a store a couple of shops down from his office. "That's the Saddle Maker. We're gonna have to get you a saddle and a horse one of these days. Don't worry. We have time."

In a few more feet we were at the Land Office. "This is where you file a deed for property you wanna buy. I don't think you'll be needing this place." He pointed across the street. "There's the Feed and Grain store. They have seed there too. It's a popular stop for farmers and ranchers."

In the window of the Feed and Grain was a sign that read *Peat Moss, twenty-five cents*. I thought to myself for a minute. Hey, that might work. That might just work. I wondered if I should bounce it off the sheriff first. I wasn't sure what he'd think about it.

"And here's the livery stable." He walked in. "Hey Jeremiah, I'd like you to meet a friend of mine. An old man in a funny straw hat appeared. He was holding a horse by the reins. Jeremiah Adams, I'd like to meet..." The sheriff paused.

I extended my hand to shake. "The name is Pete. Pete Moss."

The sheriff looked at me strangely.

"You mean like...?" Jeremiah said as he pointed to the Feed and Grain.

"Not exactly," I said. "Pete is spelled P-E-T-E."

"Oh, oh, I see," the old man said. "Well, welcome to Abilene."

"Thanks," I said.

We crossed the street. We had to wait while a couple cowboys on horseback passed by. A horse-drawn carriage followed.

"*Pete Moss*?" Sheriff Malone said. "That's what you came up with?"

"It's short and sweet...and doesn't have many vowels."

The sheriff shook his head. "Okay, it's your name."

We made our way past Halsey's Restaurant, the Abilene General Store, Mason's Haberdashery, and the Ranchview Saloon. I was most interested in the saloon. Don't get the wrong idea. I didn't drink, and I had no interest in doing so. But I knew that this was the location where Sheriff Malone would be playing poker on July 11th. And that was a dark day in my book.

We walked by a building under construction and stopped. "Pete. Should I call you Pete now? the sheriff asked.

"Yes, I guess so. I need to get used to it."

"Okay, Pete, as you can see, they're building an addition onto the bank. They're adding space for a couple more tellers and a larger vault."

I nodded. I was wondering if any outlaws would take a shot at robbing the place while construction was going on. Another step forward and I stopped abruptly.

"Oh, man, that hurts."

"What happened?" the sheriff said.

I sat down on a nearby bench and looked at the bottom of my shoe. I had managed to step on a nail, and it had gone right through one of the holes in my shoe. I slowly pulled it out. There was blood on it."

"We gotta get you over to Doc's. He can put something on that cut and bandage it up. And then we have to get over to the General Store and pick you up a pair of boots."

"I don't have any money with me," I said.

"Not a problem," Sheriff Malone said. "The boots will be courtesy of the city of Abilene. You work for the sheriff's office now."

I followed the sheriff and hobbled down the street to a small building on the outskirts of town. On the front was a shingle that read, *Thomas Conrad, M.D.* We walked in and spotted an older, white-haired man asleep on a chair in the corner of the room. This was the doctor? I was starting to get a little worried.

"Hey, Doc," the sheriff said.

The old man stirred for a moment. Then his head popped up and he opened his eyes.

"Oh, hi, Amos. What can I do for you?"

"First of all, I'd like you to meet my replacement."

"Your replacement?" the doctor said. "You going somewhere?"

"Well, actually, he's my apprentice. He'll be shadowing me for a couple of years. Then we'll see if he's ready to take over."

A couple of years? I thought I'd only be here for a few weeks. What about seventh grade? I suddenly wasn't so sure about signing up for this assignment.

"Did I see the boy just limp?" Doc Conrad said.

"Yeah, he picked up a nail near the construction site by the bank."

He patted his hand on a table in the center of the room. "Sit up here, son," the Doc said. "Let's have a look."

I hopped up on the examining table and took my shoe off.

"That's a pretty fancy shoe you got there, boy. Never seen anything like it." He looked at the bottom of the shoe. "If he keeps wearing this thing around, Amos, he'll be up here every day with a bloody foot. You ought to fix him up."

"Doc, right after this, we're headed to the General Store to pick him up some new boots."

"Well, that's good." Doc Conrad turned to me. "Take that sock off, boy." He began examining my foot. He pushed his finger into the cut.

"Ouch!"

The Doc raised his eyes to the sheriff. "The kid seems a little soft, Amos. You sure he's sheriff material?"

I didn't appreciate the comment. If I had known he

was going to jab me like that, I could have prepared myself for it.

"We'll have to toughen him up a little," the sheriff said. "But I'm sure he'll be fine."

Doc Conrad motioned to Sheriff Malone. "Hand me that bottle of alcohol, will ya." The doctor poured some alcohol onto a small cloth and wiped the cut with it.

I gritted my teeth. It really burned. I refused to utter a sound. I refused to be called *soft* twice in the same morning.

"You keep an eye on this, boy. If it gets all pussy or turns black, you come right back here. That'll mean it's infected."

"I'll make sure he watches it, Doc," the sheriff said.

The doctor proceeded to bandage it up. "That should do it."

I put my sock and shoe back on and hopped off the table. My foot actually felt a little better. I think the bandage acted like padding.

"Thank you, doctor," I said.

He shook my hand. "I hope I never see you again. Nothing personal. It's just that it's usually bad news when we get together. By the way, what's your name?"

"Pete...Pete Moss."

The doctor looked at the sheriff. "Interesting."

Sheriff Malone just smiled. "Thanks a lot, Doc."

"It's good to see you again, Amos. To be honest, it's nice to have you here under these circumstances. I'm a little tired of cleaning up your bruises or digging a bullet out of you."

What? I thought Abilene was a peaceful town. What was this about bruises and bullets?

"Be careful, Doc. We don't want to scare the boy now."

"He oughta know what he's getting himself into." Doc Conrad turned to me. "Son, sheriffing is a dangerous profession. You gotta keep your wits 'bout you at all times. And never...never turn your back on anyone. You got it?"

If this guy was trying to scare me, he was doing a pretty good job. "I got it, sir."

"Good," he said and patted me on the top of my head. "Stay safe, you two."

The sheriff winked and nodded at the doctor, and we were off.

When we were back on the street, the sheriff stopped. "Pete, don't pay any attention to Doc Conrad. He likes to exaggerate the situation. Things are pretty calm around here."

"So, why did he say those things?"

"Well, it's true. He has cleaned up a few bruises, and he has dug a bullet out of me every now and then, but it hasn't happened often."

"Okay, I guess."

He put his arm around me. "C'mon, let get you some boots." We walked down the street to the General Store. Right as we were opening the door to enter, a man came running up.

"Sheriff, there's trouble at the Ranchview. Two poker players. You gotta get over there fast."

Sheriff Malone motioned for me to follow him. "You ready for your first taste of sheriffing?"

"I guess." But I really wasn't sure I was.

CHAPTER 5

WE RAN IN THE DIRECTION OF THE SALOON. I DIDN'T KNOW if I'd be allowed in. I wasn't sure what kind of trouble was brewing. Would it be dangerous?

We burst into the saloon and found a man holding a broken beer bottle and swinging it at another man.

"Hold it right there," the sheriff said. "Put the bottle down."

"He called me a cheat," the man said. "No one calls me a cheat."

The sheriff seemed to focus his attention on the man being threatened with the broken bottle. He apparently was an Abilene resident.

"Dale, you've lived here all your life. You've never caused any problems in town before. You're an upright citizen. What's the problem?"

"He was cheatin'," Dale said. "He dealt a card from the bottom of the deck. I saw him. So, I called him out."

The sheriff walked up to the two men and stood between them. He reached down and picked up a hand of playing cards from the poker table.

"Whose cards are these?" he said.

"Those are mine," Dale said.

"You've got two pairs, queens over tens." He looked to the man holding the bottle. "What's your name?"

"Rupert...Rupert Olsen."

"Mr. Olsen, which cards are yours?"

The man pointed to the other side of the table.

The sheriff walked over and picked them up. "You've got three of a kind."

"I told ya," the man said. "I beat him fair and square. I ain't no cheat."

"Oh, really," the sheriff said. "Then explain this to me." He held up the three of a kind. Three queens. "How'd you manage to get three queens."

"They was dealt to me like that. And they all came off the top of the deck."

"There are only four queens in the entire deck," the sheriff said. "And Dale has two of them. One of these cards is a ringer."

"Maybe he has the phony queen," the stranger said. "Did you ever think of that?"

Sheriff Malone sat down at the table and examined each of the queens. He stood each of the cards up on end. One of them was just slightly taller than the other four. "And here it is. It was one of yours, Mr. Olsen."

"I told you," Dale said. "He's a cheat."

"That card came out of the deck," the man said nervously. "I didn't put it in there."

"Well, I'm sayin' you did," Sheriff Malone said. "I want you to put that bottle down...or I'll be forced to take it away from you."

"How you gonna do that? You ain't even wearin' a gun."

"I don't need a gun to handle you. I'm tellin' you for the last time—put it down."

The man looked around the bar. He didn't seem to have any supporters. Most folks were shaking their heads.

"Sure, whatever you say, Sheriff." He dropped the bottle. It crashed to the ground.

"Now listen, stranger. By all rights, I should lock you up. People don't take kindly to card sharks. You're not welcome in this town. And if you show your face within thirty miles of Abilene, I'll toss your sorry butt in jail. You got that?"

"You can't do that."

"I not only can, but I will. And I'll tell every gambler from here to Topeka that Rupert Olsen is a cheater. You won't be able to get a game anywhere in this state. Now, get out."

The man brushed up against a half dozen people as he walked to the door. "Thanks for the hospitality, Sheriff. But I gotta tell ya—this is nothin' but a lousy hick town. You haven't heard the last of me."

"Good riddance, my good man," the sheriff said.

Olsen sneered as he walked out.

As if an applause sign had lit up, every person in the saloon started cheering. Many patted Sheriff Malone on the back. When I looked around, I noticed that Jeremiah Adams, the man I had met earlier from the livery stable, had witnessed the entire showdown.

He walked over to me, leaned down, and whispered. "Now that's what you call good sheriffing, son. Problem solved and no one got hurt. That's why Lone Wolf Malone is the best. You got some big shoes to fill."

"Sheriff, I'd like to buy you a drink," Jeremiah said.

"No, let me buy him one," another man said.

Then there were more than a half dozen others all trying to treat the sheriff to a free drink.

"I'm on duty, folks," the sheriff said. "Thanks, but I'll take a pass." He looked in my direction and nodded toward the door. It was our cue to leave.

I joined the sheriff at the door and we walked out onto the street. "Sheriff, I don't know if you should have brought me back here with you."

"Now why do you say that?"

"Because I never could have done what you did back there. I wouldn't have known to check their cards like that."

"Do you think I knew that trick my first day on this job? Heck, no. I learned it from the man whose place I took—Big Mike McGee. I saw him do the same thing more than twenty years ago. Poker cheats have been using that trick for as long as there've been card games." He smiled. "So, now you know. And when you're in this job, you'll know exactly what to do."

"I don't know. You just seemed so calm. It was beautiful."

The sheriff put his hand on my shoulder. "I appreciate the compliment."

My attention was immediately drawn to a cowboy who rode up to the hitching post, hopped down, and tied up his horse. When he stepped up onto the wooden sidewalk, he inadvertently bumped into a ranch hand who was passing by.

"Watch where you're going," the ranch hand snapped.

"What are you talking about?" the cowboy said. "You bumped into me. Someone ought to teach you some manners."

"And you think *you're* gonna do that?" the ranch hand said.

The sheriff shook his head. "Back to work."

Right at that moment, I started thinking about how Sheriff Malone had broken up the fight in the bar without a punch being thrown. I liked to think that I was capable of doing the same thing someday. And why would the sheriff have invited me to Abilene to take over if he didn't think I could handle squabbles like these? I needed to show him he hadn't made a mistake by choosing me.

I grabbed the sheriff's arm. "Let me handle this.".

Sheriff Malone smiled and folded his arms. "Would you look at this. Your first day on the job and you're all ready to mix things up." He gestured toward the two men. "Be my guest."

I took a deep breath and walked up to the two men. "Excuse me, gentlemen. I couldn't help but notice that you were having a disagreement. Maybe I can help?"

"Maybe *you* can help?" the cowboy said. "You're nuthin' but a kid. Get outta here." He pushed me away.

I looked at the sheriff. He pointed back at the two men who had now made fists and were in a fighting stance. I walked back up to them.

"I don't want to be a pest, gentlemen," I said, "but can't we solve this dispute without physical violence?"

The ranch hand looked at the cowboy. "Do you know this kid?"

The cowboy shook his head.

"Son, get the heck out of here before you get hurt," the ranch hand said.

"Well, I think that if we can just talk it out," I said, "we might be able to clear things up."

Both men dropped their fists.

The cowboy turned to me. "You're nuthin' but a pain in the neck," the cowboy said.

"Yeah," the ranch hand said, "You're a pain in the neck." He turned to the cowboy. "Can you believe this kid?"

"He sure is something else," the cowboy said.

"You know what I think," the ranch hand said. "I think the two of us ought to tan his hide right here on Main Street."

I took a few steps back.

The cowboy slapped the ranch hand on the back and laughed. "Now yer talkin',"

I retreated even further. I was waiting for the sheriff to intervene.

"I like the way you think," the cowboy said. "I'd like to buy you a drink."

"I'll take you up on that," the ranch hand said.

The cowboy stared at me. "Boo!"

I jumped back.

They both laughed as they walked in the direction of the saloon.

I walked back to where the sheriff was standing. "Not very good, huh?"

"*Not very good*?! Are you kidding? You did great."

"I don't get it."

"You went over there to stop a fight from happening... and you did it."

"But now they hate me," I said.

"That's how it turns out sometimes. You just gotta be happy with a victory no matter how ugly it is." He patted me on the back. "C'mon, let's get you those boots."

We walked across the street and into the General Store. The shelves were filled with various items. A man with a handlebar mustache and his hair parted down the middle came up to us.

"Howdy, Sheriff," what can we do for you?

"Mr. Crowley, I'd like you to meet a young friend of mine—Pete Moss."

The man smiled. He had a funny expression on his face. Every time I was introduced as *Pete Moss*, people seemed to have that reaction. I was starting to wonder if I had chosen the best possible name for myself.

"It's nice to meet you, Pete," Mr. Crowley said. "What brings you in today?"

"We need a pair of boots for the young man," the sheriff said.

"Oh, I think we can handle that," Mr. Crowley said. "Follow me."

He led us to another part of the store with dozens of shoes and boots on various shelves.

"You can look through some of these. You can choose from browns and blacks, square-toed or pointed-toe, buffalo hide or cowhide. The sizes for a boy of his age are on this shelf. Take your time. Let me know when you see something you like."

"Thank you," I said.

I walked up to the boots and started looking around but my attention was soon drawn to the front counter. A young girl had walked into the store and was staring at a candy jar.

"Good morning, Abigail," Mr. Crowley said. "Are you interested in some rock candy?"

She shook her head.

The girl had on a bonnet and a long brown dress. I was having a hard time seeing her face.

"What can I get you then?" the storekeeper said.

"What I'd really like is some licorice root, but I don't think my dad will let me have it."

The girl turned toward me for a moment and my heart sank. She was beautiful. Right at that moment I couldn't care less about getting a new pair of boots, I just wanted to stare at Abigail.

"Where's your dad?" Mr. Crowley asked.

"In the saddle store," she said.

"Well, maybe he'll buy you some when he comes by."

"I don't think so."

A man in a straw hat and overalls opened the front door. "C'mon, Abigail, we have to go."

"Mr. Walker, Abigail was interested in some licorice root," Mr. Crowley said.

"She's got plenty of sweets at home," the man said. "Let's go, sweetie." I watched out the window as he jumped up onto his buckboard wagon.

"I'll buy the child some candy," an older woman with graying hair said. She was looking at a display of ribbons. "Every child should have licorice root."

"Well, I don't think her father wants her to have it," Mr. Crowley said.

"What does he know?" the woman said. "Hiram Walker takes his children for granted. He has no idea what it's like to lose a child." She turned to Abigail. "Go ahead, dear, take a piece. I'll pay for it."

"I'd better not," Abigail said. She looked at Mr. Crowley. "I have to go." She turned and ran out of the store.

"What was that all about?" I said to the sheriff.

"Find a pair of boots you like." He leaned down and whispered, "I'll tell you about that old woman back in the office."

I resumed my hunt for a pair of boots. They all looked

really great. I couldn't make up my mind. I took a peek at what the sheriff was wearing. He had on a pair of square-toed medium brown cowhide boots. If those were good enough for the finest sheriff in the land, then they were good enough for me. I picked out a pair that closely resembled the sheriff's. I sat down and tried them on. The first pair was too big. The next pair hurt my feet. Then I found the perfect fit. They felt great.

"Can I have these?" I asked.

The sheriff turned one of the boots over to see the price. He smiled. "I think the city fathers would be okay with those. Take them up to the counter."

I carried them up to the front of the store.

"Mr. Crowley, can you put these on the sheriff's office tab, please."

"You got it," he said. "These are some real nice boots, son. You're going to like them."

"I'm sure I will," I said.

The old woman came up behind us. "Who's this, Amos?"

"This is my new apprentice, Mrs. Hailey. His name is Pete."

"Would you like some licorice root, Pete?" she said.

I wasn't sure how to answer. Partly because I had never seen licorice that looked like that before. I wasn't so sure I'd like it.

"No, thank you, I'm fine," I said.

"Would you like some licorice root for yourself, Mrs. Hailey?" Mr. Crowley asked.

"Heavens no! Can't stand the taste, but I know the kids like it." She was still looking at me. "I haven't seen you around here before, young man. Who are your parents?"

The sheriff had a funny look on his face. "Oh, you

wouldn't know them. They're from Wichita. Pete is staying with me for a few days." He turned to me before the woman could ask another question. "Well, you ready to go?"

I nodded.

Mr. Crowley handed me a large box and we headed for the door.

"See you soon, sheriff," he said as we left.

We crossed the street and headed for the sheriff's office.

"So, who was that lady?" I asked.

He pointed to the office. "Wait till we're inside." He leaned closer. "It's a whopper."

I wasn't sure what all the secrecy was about, but I was sure interested in finding out.

CHAPTER 6

I SAT DOWN ON ONE OF THE BUNKS AND TRIED ON MY NEW boots. They fit perfectly, although I moved somewhat clumsily in them. It was hard to get used to how high the heels were. I walked around for a couple of minutes in the office to try to get used to them.

"Don't worry," the sheriff said. "They'll feel normal in a couple of days."

"I hope so." I sat back down. "Sheriff, you were gonna tell me about that old lady we saw in the General Store."

"Mrs. Hailey. Yeah. She's a tough old bird."

"What do you mean?"

"Her husband died about twenty years ago. That just left her and her teenage daughter, Heather. I remember I had only been on the job a couple of years when I was passing by their farm on the way back to Abilene one day. I decided to stop in to see if I could water my horse. While I was there, Heather came out of the barn with some feed for the chickens. She was carrying a pail and walking kind of unsteady. A moment later, she collapsed. I carried her into the house and laid her down. She looked bad. I remember her skin was kind of bluish. I knew something was wrong. I offered to ride into town to fetch Doc Meadows. He was the doctor in Abilene before Doc Conrad. But Mrs. Hailey would have none of it. She refused to have her daughter seen by a doctor."

"Why was that, do you suppose?"

"It had to do with her husband. He had died only a few months earlier. He had developed some sort of a blockage in his intestine. Doc Meadows told his wife that the only way to save him was to operate. But things didn't go well. Mr. Hailey died on the operating table. And since then, Mrs. Hailey has never trusted doctors. She wouldn't see them, and she wouldn't let her daughter see them."

"So, what happened to her daughter?" I asked.

"Well, I went to see Doc Meadows. I told him how the Hailey girl looked. I mentioned that her skin was kind of bluish gray. He told me that it sounded like cholera, and that she needed medical treatment right away. Doc Meadows and I went back to the farm the next day but Mrs. Hailey refused to let him treat her. There was nothing we could do. You can't force someone to accept medical help."

"I just don't get it. Even though her daughter might have died, she wouldn't let the doctor take a look at her?"

"A couple of weeks later, I decided to pay her a visit. I wanted to see how Heather was doing. When I got there, I found a freshly dug grave out behind the barn. When I asked Mrs. Hailey about it, she said her daughter had died. But the strangest thing was what came out of her mouth next. Mrs. Hailey told me that her daughter hadn't died of cholera. Instead, she said that she had been killed by Indians."

"What?"

"That's what I thought. We hadn't had an Indian raid around here for years. Most of the tribes in the area were now on reservations. We were at peace. When I asked her how she knew it was Indians, she said that she had been out in the fields when she saw three braves near her house. When she got back, Heather was dead."

"How come she never reported it?"

"That's the first thing I thought. If there was a war party in the area, you'd want to let your neighbors know."

"Do you think she was telling the truth?" I asked.

"Not in the slightest. Doc Meadows and I were convinced that she made up the story to cover the fact that she hadn't sought out any medical treatment for her daughter's cholera. It was easier to say that she had been killed by Indians."

Every time I heard the sheriff use the word *Indians*, I cringed. He wasn't aware that we now referred to these people as Native Americans or Indigenous Americans.

"It wasn't very nice accusing the Indians of something they didn't do," I said.

"It really made me mad," Sheriff Malone said. "The White man has done terrible things to Indian tribes all over this country. We stole lands that they had settled and called them our own. Those tribes were the rightful owners of those lands, but we saw fit to strip them of it. Then we stuck them on these god-awful reservations. Heck, those places are nothing more than prison camps. And where did we put 'em? Nowhere near any rivers or streams, and nowhere near where buffalo herds graze. Then when they leave the reservations to hunt or fetch water, we accuse them of violating the agreement they made with the government. It's an awful state of affairs. We should be ashamed of ourselves."

I was really glad to hear that the sheriff was a real supporter of the Native American cause. I had a bad feeling though that there weren't many other people who felt the way he did.

"So, that's the story of Mrs. Hailey," he said. "You can probably tell I'm not one of her biggest fans."

"Hey, Sheriff," a voice said from the cell area.

"Time to free our prisoner," the sheriff said. He got up and walked back to where the cells were located. He grabbed a set of keys off the wall, unlocked the cell, and swung the door open. "Are you ready to become a contributing member of society, Hank?" he said to the man.

"I learned my lesson, sheriff. I ain't never gonna have another drink."

"You don't have to go that far. We're not the temperance police. Just know your limit and try to keep from bustin' up the place."

"You don't have to worry, sheriff. I learned my lesson."

"I'm glad to hear that. I hate to tell you this, Hank, but you did about fifty dollars worth of damage over at the saloon. You're gonna have to pay that back."

"You think they'll let me pay a little bit each week?"

"I'm sure Dolly will be happy to work out a payment plan."

Hank motioned to me. "Who's your friend?"

"This is Pete Moss. He's learning the sheriffing business."

"You're learning from the best, boy," he said to me.

"Oh, I know that," I said.

It seemed like wherever we went, people had nothing

but nice things to say about this sheriff. It made me think more about what would happen a month from now at that poker game. I knew the sheriff had warned me about telling him what would take place in the future—because it would change the course of history. But so what? What if a few things turned out differently because Amos Malone was still alive? How could that be a bad thing? I would just have to wait for the right moment to tell him.

When Hank had left, I decided to try again. "Sheriff, can I ask you a question?"

"Sure."

"If you knew you only had one month to live, are there any things you would want to do before you died?"

"Where did that come from?"

"I was just wondering."

"Well, to tell you the truth, I've never thought about it much. I guess..." He stopped and stared at me. "Wait a minute. Pete, what did I tell you about the future? You can't tell me what's going to happen. Even if it's bad."

"It is bad, Sheriff. It's a case of life and death."

He put his hands over his ears. "I'm not listening."

"You are so stubborn."

"Pete, you can't change history. If I thought you were going to try to do that, I would never have brought you here. Once and for all, this conversation is over. Understood?"

I nodded reluctantly. I had to figure out a way to warn him. I refused to let Lone Wolf Malone die on July 11th at the Ranchview Saloon. I just refused.

"Well, you ready to grab a bite to eat?" the sheriff asked. "The dining room's small. It fills up fast. We'd better step on it."

We walked over to Halsey's Restaurant. And just as the sheriff had predicted, every table was in use.

"Dang it," Sheriff Malone said. Then he spotted someone. "Wait here."

I watched as he walked across the dining room and stopped at a table. I couldn't see who was sitting there but whoever it was, he was sitting alone. A moment later, the sheriff waved me over. As I got closer, I could see the man was Doc Conrad.

"Doc has generously invited us to share his table," the sheriff said.

"Well, how's that foot, Pete?" Doc Conrad asked.

"Just fine, thanks."

"Good, glad to hear it." The doctor motioned to the waiter.

A minute later, he brought over two menus. When I opened it, I couldn't believe the prices. Beef steak, ten cents; pork chops, ten cents, fried halibut, ten cents, fried ham, ten cents. How could this place possibly make any money?

"I'll have the fried halibut," the sheriff said. "And a cup of coffee."

"And you, young man?" the waiter asked.

The sheriff jumped out of his chair and began smashing something on the floor with his boot. He did it two or three times. He turned to the waiter.

"Can you ask Fred to come out here for a minute," the sheriff asked.

"Yes, sir." He looked at me. "You were saying."

"Um...fried ham and a glass of milk, please."

"Very good." The waiter took our menus and left.

"Busy day, Doc?" the sheriff said.

"Today wasn't bad but I've got a long day tomorrow."

"Oh, yeah?"

"I have to go out to the Walker farm. That's a good twenty miles. The little boy there, Tommy, broke his arm about six weeks ago. I have to remove the cast."

Walker? Why did that sound familiar? And then it hit me. "Does Tommy have an older sister by any chance?" I asked.

"Abigail," the doctor said.

"Oh, okay."

The sheriff chuckled. "You don't fool me, Pete."

"What?" I said.

The sheriff leaned toward Doc Conrad. "Pete couldn't take his eyes off of Abigail earlier today at the General Store."

"That's not true," I said. I knew I was turning red.

"It's perfectly all right, son," Doc said. "Abigail is a very pretty girl." The doctor thought to himself for a moment. "You know, Amos, if Pete wants to, he could join me tomorrow morning when I go over there. It'd be kind of nice to have some company on the ride." He turned to me. "Would you like to come? We leave at seven."

I looked at the sheriff. "Is it okay?"

"How could I stand in the way of true love?" the sheriff said.

Doc Conrad chuckled.

"Aw, Sheriff," I said.

"I'm just foolin' with you, Pete," he said. "You go with the doc. You might learn something."

A man in a gray suit appeared at the table. "What'd you need, Sheriff?"

"Fred, I had to kill a half dozen cockroaches when I came in here."

Fred made a face. "Get used to it. Every business in Abilene has cockroaches."

"But these were bigger," Sheriff Malone said.

"What do you expect?" the man said. "The food here is better."

The sheriff and Doc Conrad laughed.

"I see," the sheriff said. "The bigger, the better. Huh?"

"Something like that," Fred said. He looked at me. "Who's your dinner companion?"

"This is Pete Moss. He'd like to become a sheriff someday. So, he's following me around to see if he'll like it."

"What do you think, Pete?" Fred said.

"It's pretty exciting," I said. "There's always something going on."

"Just be careful," he said. "Someone tried to hold us up about two weeks ago. The sheriff happened to be sitting right over there." He pointed across the room. "And Amos here had the man in handcuffs and behind bars before dessert was served. You'll learn a lot from this fellow."

"I know. I already am."

"Was that it, Sheriff? You just wanted to lecture me about the cockroach infestation?"

"That was about it."

The two men smiled. I listened to the sheriff and Doc shoot the breeze before and during dinner. When the food finally came, I had to admit it wasn't bad. But how could you complain about anything that cost so little? When we finished, the sheriff and I walked around town for a little while. He told me about some of the adventures from his younger days. They seemed exciting *and* dangerous. The more I listened, the more I worried about being a sheriff in the Old West. It almost seemed as if you took your life into your own hands on a daily basis. And which day would an angry, deranged gambler make it your last? Sheriff Malone didn't know what I knew. He'd know soon enough if I had anything to do with it. Even though he forbid me from telling him, I just had to. It would probably be the first and last time I would disobey him.

CHAPTER 7

I HAD A HARD TIME SLEEPING THAT NIGHT. I WASN'T SURE IF it was the paper-thin mattress or my excitement about seeing Abigail again. It was difficult to get comfortable. Besides little to no padding, the bunks were really narrow. If you were a restless sleeper, there was a pretty good chance you'd end up falling out onto the floor. I made it a point to hug the wall. I noticed that something was digging into my thigh. I reached into my pocket and pulled out the magnet I had taken from my locker at school. I wasn't sure how useful it would be here with most things made of wood. I slid it back into my pocket but positioned it so it wasn't jabbing me. The sheriff had let me use a crude, wind-up alarm clock so I'd wake up on time in order to go with Doc to the Walker farm in the morning. The ticking was so loud it was hard to sleep. Maybe that was how this thing worked—it just kept you awake all night so you wouldn't miss an important appointment. Apparently, I did manage to fall asleep though because I was awakened with a thud at six thirty by an ear-piercing alarm. It unfortunately woke up the sheriff too.

"I'm sorry," I said as I tried to turn off the alarm. I kept pushing buttons and levers, but nothing seemed to work. Eventually the sheriff got up and turned it off. "You go back to sleep," I said. "I'll be real quiet."

"Don't worry about it, Pete. Once I down a cup of coffee, I'll be fine."

"Sorry again."

The sheriff opened a cabinet and produced two stale muffins that had to have been in there for a couple of days.

"Here, chow down. You don't have enough time for breakfast at Halsey's."

As I chomped down on the rock-hard muffin, I was surprised I didn't crack a tooth. It all made me kind of homesick. I began thinking about the kind of breakfast I could have had if I had stayed home—pancakes, scrambled eggs, pork sausages, fresh-squeezed orange juice. I had to stop thinking like that. It would make me crazy.

At six-fifty-five, I headed over to Doc Conrad's office. He was busy making sure he had packed all the instruments he would need to remove a cast.

"Did you have something to eat?" he asked.

"Yeah, I had a muffin."

"Three-day-old stale muffins?"

"Something like that."

"I'll bet it was real tasty," he said sarcastically.

"It *was* a little hard."

He walked over to a small wooden box and pulled out a piece of bread. He placed it on the hot stove for a minute and then loaded it with honey.

"Here," he said. "This'll get the taste of that muffin out of your mouth."

I bit into it and couldn't believe how delicious it was. "This is so much better."

He laughed. "Amos is a fine sheriff, but his cooking skills leave something to be desired." Doc Conrad closed up his case and put on his jacket. "Y'all ready?"

I nodded. We walked outside and hopped into his one-horse buggy. I pointed to the horse.

"What's his name?"

"That's Clementine," he said. We've been together for a lot of years now. But she's getting close to retirement age. I'll miss her when she's gone." He shook the reins and we were off. The ride was a lot bumpier than I was expecting. Shock absorbers would have helped. I was surprised Doc Conrad didn't seem to mind it when we were bounced a foot up in the air when we hit a hole in the road. He just smiled and talked to Clementine.

"You're doing great, girl. Just a few more miles." He turned to me. "You know, Pete, I don't know much about you. Where are you from?"

Uh oh. I didn't think *the future* would be the best response. I had to think fast. I needed a town somewhere in Kansas to make it believable. Then I remembered how the sheriff had answered that question the day before.

"I'm from Wichita."

"Wichita, huh? That's about a three days ride from here. Your folks there?"

"Yeah."

"What's your pa do?"

"He's um...he's a farmer."

"What does he raise?"

"You know, just the basic crops...peas and beans and carrots." I had to get this man on another topic. I had lied more in the last five minutes than I had in my entire life. "So, Doc, do you have any exciting stories? Like how many bullets you've dug out of lawmen in your career."

He looked at me and smiled. "Now that's kind of grim, don't you think?

"Well, I didn't mean it like that. I was just wondering if you had any really exciting things happen to you, that's all." I was blowing it. I soon realized I didn't know how to talk to someone who lived in the 1880s. After all the Old West books I had read and movies I had seen, you would think I'd be better at this. I guess because this was real life and not some book or TV show, I didn't really know what I was doing.

"Let me see. There must be something you'd find interesting. How about the time little Mikey Leach stuffed a plateful of peas up his nose?"

"Did that really happen?"

"As sure as I'm sittin' here. Or the time five-year-old Doris Martin swallowed a silver dollar?"

"That sounds a little hard to believe."

"True story. Pete, did you ever hear the phrase, *in one ear and out the other*?"

"Sure, everyone has."

"Well, little Jonah Masters was so sure that statement was true, he took a pencil, stuck the pointy end in one ear, and jammed it as hard as he could. He was so sure it would come out the other ear." He smiled. "Are those the kinds of stories you're looking for?"

"Well, yeah, I guess."

"Okay, then, back to Mikey Leach and the pea story..."

And so, for the remainder of the ride to the Walker farm, Doc Conrad told me the strangest tales I had ever heard—the peas story, the silver dollar story, the pencil story, and a few others. I just sat there with my mouth open. About fifty minutes later, a farmhouse came into view.

"Is that it?" I said.

"Sure is. And if you look closely, you can see Mr. Walker tending his crops."

I looked for a few seconds before I was able to spot the man Doc was referring to. He wore long overalls, a white tee shirt, a straw hat, and a red kerchief tied around his neck. As we got closer, he waved to us. Doc guided the carriage up to the farmhouse and pulled back on the reins.

"Whoa, Clementine, this is it, darlin'."

We hopped out and waited next to the carriage for a moment. Mr. Walker ran up from behind.

"Hi, Doc," he said.

"Morning, Hiram. It's a beautiful day, isn't it?"

"Sure is," Mr. Walker said. He stared at me momentarily.

"Oh, this is my friend, Pete. He came along to assist me."

"He's more than welcome. Well, come on in. Martha just took some rolls out of the oven."

"So, where's our patient?" Doc asked.

"He and Abby are inside," Mr. Walker said. He led us into the house. We entered through the kitchen. Tommy was sitting at the table eating breakfast. Abigail was wearing an apron. She didn't have on a bonnet this time. She had long brown hair that hung down to the middle of her back. When she saw me, she smiled and looked away.

"Sit down, Doc," Mrs. Walker said. "Would you like some coffee?"

"That sounds real good," Doc said. He noticed Mrs. Walker looking at me. "This is my assistant, Pete."

She smiled. "Would you like anything to eat or drink, son?"

"No, thank you." I spotted Abigail staring at me. I was hoping she wouldn't turn away like last time. She was so pretty. I really enjoyed looking at her. I suddenly heard a sound at my feet. When I looked down, there was a small dog growling at me. I couldn't help but notice that the dog had only three legs.

"Don't mind him," Mrs. Walker said. "He's Abby's dog. He's just protecting her." She leaned over toward the dog. "He's a friend, Killer. Be nice to him."

"Killer?" I said.

Abigail laughed.

Her mother smiled. "That's the name Abby gave him. She figured the name might discourage anyone who tried to bother her."

"But he only has three legs," I said.

"Don't that let fool you," her mother said. "He still packs a pretty good punch. But, truly, he's a softie at heart. Before you leave, he'll be licking your hand."

"Just don't say the magic word," Abby said.

"The magic word?" I replied.

"If you say it and point to someone, he'll attack."

"So, what's the magic word?" I said. "Just so I know not to say it."

"You'd better whisper it to him, Abby," her mother said.

Abby walked over and leaned in. "It's *Nonoma*." She

pulled back. "Just don't say it unless you know what you're doing."

"What does it mean?" I asked.

"It's the Cheyenne word for *thunder*."

"Have you ever said it out loud?" I said.

"One time," her mother said. "When a coyote attacked the chickens. Abby pointed to the coyote, said the word, and Killer did the rest."

"That critter ran off with his tail between his legs," Abby said.

"I'm a believer," I said. "I won't mess with Killer."

They all laughed.

"Well, Tommy," Doc said. "Are you ready to get that nasty thing off your arm?"

"I kinda like it," he said.

"Don't listen to him, Doc," Mrs. Walker said. "He's gotten that thing so filthy, I'll be thrilled when it's gone."

Tommy lifted his cast and pulled it up against his chest. "Cut it off?"

"How else do you think it'll come off, silly?" his mother said.

"Is it gonna hurt?" he said.

"Oh, don't be such a baby," Abigail said.

"All right, Abby. We'll have none of that," her mother said.

"I'll tell you what, Martha. Put that coffee on hold for a minute. Let's get that cast off and then we can all relax. How's that sound?"

"Fine with me," Mrs. Walker said.

Doc leaned over, opened his case, and pulled out a small handheld saw.

Tommy jumped up and ran to his mother. "He's gonna use *that*?"

"I promise it won't hurt a bit," Doc said. "I've done this hundreds of times and no one has ever felt a thing." He scratched. "Of course, there was that time I cut off Ethan Baker's left hand by mistake."

Tommy bolted for the door. Mrs. Walker dragged him back to the table.

"I'm just kidding, Tommy," the doc said, laughing.

"I don't want her in here," Tommy said, pointing at Abigail.

"Fine with me," she said.

"I don't want anybody in here," the youngster said. "Just Doc."

"Not even me?" his mom said.

"Well, okay, but just you."

"Abby, why don't you show Pete around the farm," Mrs. Walker said. "Can you do that?"

"I guess." She untied her apron and hung it on the wall. "This way," she said as she walked to the front door. We walked outside and stopped. Killer followed us. "Well, what do you wanna see?"

"Everything."

"I don't mean to be rude," she said, "but who are you exactly?"

I smiled. "I came to Abilene from Wichita. That's where my folks live." Here came more lies, I thought. "I'm staying with Sheriff Malone. I'm kind of like an apprentice. He plans on retiring in the near future and he wanted to teach me the ropes."

"*Teach you the ropes?* How old are you?" she asked.

"Twelve. How about you?"

"Same."

"Cool," I said.

"Cool? What's that supposed to mean? It must be eighty-eight degrees out here."

I was getting careless. I had to remember it was 1888. "I just meant it was nice that we were the same age."

"So, when are you going back to Wichita? The end of the summer?"

"Yeah, probably."

"Oh. Well, we might as well start the tour. Let's head to the barn."

I followed her into what had to be one of the foul-smelling places I had ever been in. It reminded me of when we went into the large animal houses at the zoo.

She pointed to the first stall. "That's Butterfly. She's kind of my horse but everybody rides her some." We moved over to where two cows stood together. "That's Harriet and that one's Ruth. I have to milk them every morning."

"That sounds neat."

"Why would say that? There's nothing neat about this place. It's a mess."

I had done it again. "I just meant it sounded like fun."

"Fun. I don't think so. I have to get up at four thirty every morning. What time do you get up?"

"Six thirty this morning."

"Oh, how I would love to sleep in till six thirty."

This was another part of the Old West that didn't sound very exciting. If getting up at six thirty was *sleeping in*, I wasn't sure how long I'd survive here.

"Follow me," she said. We walked outside and went around to the side of the barn. "Here's the chicken coop. And around here..." I followed her to the back of the barn. "...are the hogs. I feed them too."

"You do a lot of work around here," I said.

"I don't really think about it. It's just always been that way."

Our attention was suddenly drawn to someone in a buckboard approaching the farmhouse.

"Oh, no," Abigail said. "It's her again."

"Who's her?"

"Mrs. Hailey."

And as she got closer, I recognized her from the General Store. "I know her," I said. "I saw her in the store yesterday. She was trying to buy me some candy."

"Me too," Abigail said. "She won't leave us alone. She must stop by here every week. She always wants to take me and Tommy places. But we don't want to go. And, fortunately, our parents don't make us."

"Maybe she's just lonely," I said. "She did lose a daughter a few years back."

"Everybody knows that story," she said. "Her daughter had Scarlet Fever or something and she wouldn't let her see a doctor."

"I heard it was cholera."

"Whatever it was, she only has herself to blame."

Mrs. Hailey's buckboard was getting closer. Killer started to growl.

"It looks like she's coming over here," I said.

"I need some excuse to make her go away."

"Why don't you just say you're showing me around."

"Perfect."

"Whoa," Mrs. Hailey said to her horse. "Well, hello, Abigail, would you like to go for a ride today?"

"No, thank you," Abigail said. "I'm afraid I'm with a guest right now."

"How about after that?"

"Well...um...I have a lot of chores to do. Sorry."

"Parents who make their kids do chores are plum lazy," the old woman said.

Abigail stared at her shoes and said nothing.

"You're Pete, right?" Mrs. Hailey said.

"Yes."

"Would you like to join me for a ride in the country?"

"Thanks very much but I'm actually here with Doc Conrad. We'll be heading back to town soon. Maybe next time."

"Maybe next time," she said. "It's a date then." She grabbed the reins. "You take care, kids." A moment later, she was gone.

"She gives me the creeps," Abigail said. She turned in the direction of the farmhouse. "Well, that's about it for the tour. Not much else to see."

"Thanks for showing me around," I said. "It was very educational."

"Educational? You're funny," she said. "By the way, if you want, you can call me Abby."

You can call me Abby. Did she actually say that? It had to mean that she liked me, or, at least, she could stand to be around me. Whatever, I'd take it.

When we went back in the house, Killer followed us back in. We found Doc Conrad cleaning off Tommy's arm. He had apparently survived the trauma of having his cast removed although I could see a tear streaming down his cheek.

"Did he cry?" Abby said.

"Now leave your brother alone," her mother said. "He handled it like a real man, right, Doc?"

"He certainly did," Doc said.

While Doc was putting his instruments away, I found myself staring at Abby. I knew this visit was about to come to an end. I didn't know when I'd see her again. As we rode back to town, I remember Doc talking to me about something, but to tell you the truth, I couldn't recall a single word he said. My mind was somewhere else. And no matter how hard I tried, I just couldn't get that girl out of my head.

when you get there, don't . . . I'd see her again. We've had Halsey's at Thompson's. Don't bring to my home . . . just to tell you the truth. I couldn't recall a single word he said. My brain was empty when she... you'd know how hard I tried. I couldn't figure out what to do.

CHAPTER 8

AFTER ABOUT A WEEK, I HAD GOTTEN INTO A SCHEDULE OF sorts. Every morning the sheriff and I would rise at about seven a.m. We'd get cleaned up and then head over to Halsey's for breakfast. That was one of my favorite times of the day. The breakfast menu there was awesome— scrambled eggs, potatoes, sausage, and toast with marmalade. Then we'd head back to the office and I would sweep out the place. The sheriff never made me sweep out the jail if there was a someone in there, but most days there weren't. And when there was, the prisoners were usually cowboys who had too much to drink the night before. They were fairly harmless. A couple of days ago, the sheriff took me to the General Store and bought me some socks, three shirts, two pairs of pants, a couple of kerchiefs, some underwear, and my own official cowboy hat. There was a lady down the street who was being paid by the sheriff's office to do our laundry, so I didn't have to worry about changing too often.

It had been a while since I had seen Abby. If she had

come into Abilene the last few days, I hadn't noticed. And I was doing my best to notice. I kept my eye on the General Store as often as possible. I hated to think I might be headed home without ever seeing her again. I wouldn't be able to deal with that. The last time we had seen each other, she had told me I could call her *Abby*. That was great news. Maybe I was softening her up. I thought she kinda liked me, but I wasn't sure. I needed to see her again to find out. I wished the sheriff had had a reason to go out to their farm for something but there just wasn't one. The day before I had even asked Doc if he thought he should go out there to see how Tommy's arm was doing, but he said that if they needed him, they'd probably bring the youngster into town.

That particular day I was pinning wanted posters on the wall in the office when the sheriff walked in with a smile on his face.

"It's that time, Pete."

"Time for what?"

"It's about time we got you your own transportation."

"Transportation?" I asked.

"Pete, today you're getting your own horse. C'mon."

I followed him down the street to the livery stable. When we walked in, Jeremiah was feeding the horses.

"Morning, sheriff, what can I do for you?" he said.

"Jeremiah, how you fixed for horses these days? It's time for my friend to have one of his own."

"I traded for a couple of nice ones yesterday. They're right over here."

We walked to the end of the stable.

"Look at these beauties," he said.

There were two horses—a black one with a white

streak just above his nose, and a chocolate brown one. The sheriff walked over and began inspecting each one of them.

"These are beautiful animals," the sheriff said. "What do you want for them?"

"I need at least fifty for the black one, and I'd settle for forty for the brown one."

I didn't care which one we chose. I'd be happy riding either one of them.

"That's a little steep, don't you think?" the sheriff said.

"Amos, I'll go down five dollars on each one but that's the best I can do."

"Pete, what do you think?" the sheriff said.

"I don't know," I said. "Either one would be great."

"If you're buying this for the boy," Jeremiah said, "I should tell you that both these horses ran wild a couple of months ago. They may still need some breakin' in."

The sheriff thought to himself for a moment. "I'll tell you what we're gonna do. I'll give my horse to Pete. She's all broken in. And I'll take one of these beauties for myself."

"That'd work," Jeremiah said. "What's your pleasure, Sheriff?"

"I think I'm gonna treat myself to the black one."

"Good choice."

"Jeremiah, can you put my saddle on the new one."

"Sure."

"And would you by any chance have an old saddle lying around that Pete could use till we get him one for himself?"

"I'll tell you what," the old man said, "Throw in an extra five dollars and I'll give you an old saddle I have lying around. It has a few miles on it, but it'd be perfect for a new rider."

"It's a deal," Sheriff Malone said.

"We'll pick them up in a few minutes and then head out for Pete's first riding lesson. Thanks, Jeremiah. And, by the way, just put that on the office charge."

"I'll do that, Amos. See you in a few minutes."

We killed time walking up and down Main Street looking for trouble. Fortunately, we hadn't found any. A little while later, we returned to find both horses rubbed down, fed, and saddled up.

"Are you ready for this?" the sheriff said.

"I guess so."

Sheriff Malone grabbed the reins of both horses and walked them to an open area behind the livery stable.

"Pete, have you ever ridden a horse before?"

I shook my head.

"Okay, let's start at the beginning. Here's the proper way to mount a horse." He stood on the left side of his horse about even with the front of the saddle. "First, you grab the reins, and then the horn of the saddle. You slip your left foot into the stirrup, and lift yourself up onto the animal. Then swing your right foot over and slide it into the other stirrup. Watch me."

I watched as the sheriff mounted his new horse. Even though I had never gotten up onto a horse in my life, I had seen enough westerns to have a pretty good idea of how to do it.

"Okay, now you try."

I walked over to my very own horse. I still couldn't believe I was saying that. I reached up and took hold of the reins. Then I grabbed the horn. I placed my left foot in the stirrup, pulled on the horn, and lifted myself up. That part had gone well. But I unfortunately put so much oomph into lifting myself up and over that all I managed to do was propel myself over the horse and ended up falling onto the ground on the other side.

The sheriff chuckled. "You okay?"

"Yeah, I think so."

"Try it again, but try to do so a little more gracefully this time. Don't pull on that horn so hard. You're not tryin' to pull the saddle off, you're just using it for leverage. You think you got it?"

I nodded.

"Okay, let's see you do it."

I had made a complete fool of myself. I wondered if the sheriff was kicking himself for bringing me back to Abilene with him. There had to have been a more worthy candidate out there than me. But I had to reassure him that I was worth the risk. I got up off my butt, walked back over to the other side of the horse, grabbed the reins, and then the horn. I slid my left foot into the stirrup, pulled down and lifted myself up. Then I swung my right foot over and slipped it into the right stirrup. I had done it. I couldn't believe it. I had actually mounted a horse.

"Well done," the sheriff said. "Now we have to teach you how to actually ride him. First, I want you to keep your heels down. From the knees down, you're not making any contact with the horse when you're not moving. Now sit a little more forward. You have to sit on what we call your seat bones, not your butt. Keep your shoulders over your hips."

And on and on. I learned every aspect of riding a horse—how to turn left; how to turn right; how to make her walk; how to make her trot; how to make her gallop; how to stop; how to make the horse walk backward; how to make her move sideways, etc. We had spent a couple of hours behind the livery stable. It was hot and getting hotter. We stopped for an occasional water break. My legs were getting sore, as was my butt. I was so glad when the sheriff announced that we had finished our lesson for the day, and it was now time for lunch. We drifted over to Halsey's for a satisfying meal including two glasses of lemonade.

We made our way back to the office and relaxed for a few minutes before the door swung open and two big, burly, hairy individuals walked in.

"Sheriff, you gotta do something," one of the men said.

"Slow down, fellas," the sheriff said. "First of all, tell me who you are?"

"I'm Josiah Hagen," the taller man said, "and this is my brother, Abe."

"Okay, so what can I do for you gentlemen?"

By their appearance, it was doubtful anyone had ever referred to this pair as gentlemen before.

"Sheriff, you gotta do something about them savages," Josiah said.

"What are you talking about? Indians?"

I hated hearing how people referred to Native Americans. It was cruel and it was unfair. They hadn't done anything to deserve that. We took away *their* lands, and somehow *they* were the bad guys. It just wasn't right.

"We was just out huntin' buffalo when a half dozen redskins were all around us," Josiah said. "We barely got away."

"They was off the reservation," Abe said. "You gotta do something."

"And why do you suppose they were there?" the sheriff said.

"They was huntin' buffalo too, I guess," Josiah said.

"I don't see what the big deal is," the sheriff said. "There's plenty of buffalo for them and for us."

"But, sheriff, they was off their reservation," Abe repeated. "They had no business out there."

"No business?!" Sheriff Malone said. "Don't you think they need the buffalo meat to feed their families, and the hides to make clothing?"

"Yeah," Josiah said, "but they didn't belong there. Don't you get it?"

"Trust me, I get it," he said. "What do you expect me to do?"

"You gotta form a posse and go after them," Abe said. "Drive 'em back to where they belong, or better yet, kill 'em."

The sheriff rubbed his forehead. "What you two learned gentlemen don't seem to realize is that when the government put the Indians on reservations, they conveniently forgot to put them on lands with water or with game. The Indians have no choice but to leave the reservation to hunt. What do you expect me to do—call in the Cavalry to force them back onto their reservations? That would be a total waste of manpower. There's no reason we can't all live in harmony."

"Why you're nuthin' but a doggone Injun lover. That's what you are," Josiah said. "And if you don't wanna do your job, then we'll have to do it for you. When we pass Fort Dodge, we're gonna tell the major what we saw. And you just watch. They'll do the right thing." He turned to his brother. "C'mon, Abe, let's get outta here. This sheriff ain't no help." The pair headed out and slammed the door behind them.

"Well, there goes a couple of fools," Sheriff Malone said.

"You did the right thing, Sheriff," I said.

He smiled. "Well, I'm glad to hear you say that."

"The Native Amer—er, the Indians were the first citizens of this country. They have as much right to the land as anyone else. More, actually."

"Pete, why can't people think like you? I've been at odds with everyone in this territory for years. No one can see things from the perspective of the Indians. If you were here first, and you settled these lands, you'd be pretty upset if a bunch of folks with guns just happened to show up and tried to drive you off."

"Sheriff, how does the Cavalry fit into all of this? And how long would it take these two to make it to Fort Dodge and tell them about it?"

"It's the Cavalry's job to see that the Indians stay on the reservations. If they wander off, the Cavalry has to round them up and take them back. But don't worry. It's about two hundred miles from Abilene to Fort Dodge. It would take those buffalo hunters a good week to get there. But personally, I think they were bluffing. I don't think they have any intention of going there. They're just trying to get me to go out to the reservation and have a talk with the chief. But I ain't going. They didn't do anything wrong."

"But what if they weren't bluffing? What if they do report this to the Cavalry? Would the troops come all the way out here just to chase the Indians back?"

"I doubt it," he said. "Now if the Indians were to form a war party, and if they burned out the settlers, or worse, killed them, then that's different. They'd be out here in a heartbeat."

"But, sheriff, who knows what these guys'll tell them. They don't want to have to compete with the Indians for buffalo. That's obvious. They could make up any kind of story. They could say that they *did* see a war party. Isn't there any way we could get to a major or a captain or someone before they do?"

The sheriff stroked his unshaven face. "Pete, I like the way you think. Now I *know* I made the right choice. You're starting to act like a sheriff—like a peacemaker. There *is* a way to get to the major first. We'll send him a telegram and tell him our side of the story."

"Can we fib a little?"

"Why not? We'll tell him that someone reported seeing a handful of Indians hunting buffalo off the reservation. Now that's the truth. Here comes the fib. I think I'll say that I went out to the Cheyenne reservation and spoke to Chief White Deer. I'll say we came to an agreement, and everything is just fine. What do you think?"

"It's perfect," I said.

He opened his desk drawer and pulled out a piece of paper and a pencil. He started writing, then looked up.

"How did I say it again?"

"You were going to say that someone reported seeing a handful of Indians hunting buffalo off the reservation. So, you went to speak to the Cheyenne chief and the two of you came to an understanding. And so now everything is fine."

"Pete, what would I do without you? Just for that, I'm going to buy you dinner."

"But you buy me dinner every night."

"Oh, yeah, so I do." He smiled and pointed at me. "Tonight, we're having dessert. How's that sound?"

"Great."

"Okay, give me a chance to write this out."

The sheriff spent the next few minutes writing the text of his telegram. When he finished, we walked across the street to the telegraph office. Then we headed to Halsey's for dinner. All I could think about was what I'd get for dessert. It was one of the first times I was actually thinking about something other than Abby.

CHAPTER 9

SEVERAL DAYS HAD PASSED SINCE THE BUFFALO HUNTERS HAD come into the office. Hopefully all of that had quieted down. By this point, I had pretty much settled into a daily routine. I was starting to get used to life in the Old West. But I did have to say that I missed some of the conveniences of home. I was okay with no automobiles. I was enjoying riding a horse, and occasionally a horse and buggy. I was fine with no cell phones. Since I didn't have one of my own, there was nothing to miss. My parents had refused to get me a cell phone until I was in high school. I did miss the internet a little. Abilene had a one-room library with very few selections. It was a bit difficult to keep up with what was going on. Thankfully there was a weekly newspaper, the *Abilene Weekly Reflector*. That helped keep me up to date on current events.

I was still having a hard time getting used to using an outhouse. We had one behind the sheriff's office. Every time I went in there, I had to hold my nose. The stench was nauseating. But since there were no other options, there wasn't much I could do about it. I did have to say that the thing I missed the most was air conditioning. The days were hot and long on the Kansas prairies. There weren't many trees. There was no way to hide from it. And the nights were even worse. It was so hot and stuffy in the sheriff's office that I could barely stand it. Every morning I would wake up completely soaked in sweat. But as uncomfortable as that was, I was on a mission, and I wasn't ready to head home until my job here was done. And I wasn't in any hurry.

Maybe that all had to do with Abby. I hadn't seen her in nearly two weeks. Since I wasn't sure how long I'd be here, I was anxious to see her again. The thought of going back home and not talking to her at least one more time made me a little crazy. We had gotten along so well the last time we were together that I was sure she was starting to like me. But there was no way the relationship could continue if we never saw each other again. Then again, she may have forgotten all about me by now. I would have to find a reason for the sheriff to go out there, but I just couldn't think of anything. Of course, maybe I could go out there myself. I had a horse now. And I pretty much knew how to ride it. There was no reason I couldn't head out there and pay her a visit. But I wasn't completely sure how to find the farm. I hadn't paid much attention to the directions we had taken before. I needed the sheriff to take me out there at least one more time before I'd feel comfortable heading there by myself.

That morning was like all the others. We had just gotten back from breakfast at Halsey's. I had tried something different today—a stack of flapjacks. I noticed that the syrup was thicker and richer here than the syrup at home. It was more like a dessert than a breakfast. Later I swept up the jail cell area and did some other chores for the remainder of the morning. I was starting to think about lunch when I heard the door open.

"Sheriff, Sheriff, where are you?" a voice said.

The sheriff came out of the back room. "What is it, Hiram?" It was Hiram Walker, Abby's father.

"They're gone! They're gone!"

"Who's gone?"

"My children. Someone's taken them. And who knows what they've done to them."

By this time, I had joined the others in the main part of the office.

"Hiram, sit down for a minute," the sheriff said.

He began pacing. "I can't sit down. I'm sick with worry. Who would do such a thing?"

The sheriff guided Mr. Walker into a chair. "Where have you looked?"

"Everywhere in the house and the barn and the fields. They're nowhere to be seen. I asked a couple of the other farmers if they had seen them, but they hadn't. I just don't know what to do."

"Are there any places where Abby and Tommy like to go when they're alone?"

"I checked the fishing hole. There was no sign of them."

"How's Martha doing?"

"She's so sick about this, I had to put her to bed. Sheriff, I need your help."

"Don't worry, we'll do everything we can to find them."

I was starting to get sick to my stomach thinking about someone hurting Abby. I imagined myself tearing them apart if I ever found them.

"Sheriff, I heard about what those buffalo hunters were talking about a while back. Do you think they were carried off by Indians?"

"They've never come this far off the reservation before. I doubt if that could have happened."

"Will you go out there? Will you go out to the reservation and look for them?"

The sheriff sighed. "Even though I don't think we'll find them there, I'll ride out and check."

Mr. Walker turned to me. "You're a friend of Abby's. Did she say anything to you about going anywhere?"

"No, sir, she didn't say anything like that."

"Can you form a posse, Sheriff? Can you do so right away?"

"I'll want to go out to check some of the farms and ranches in the area first before we do that. I'll take Pete with me. Then if we've had no luck, we'll head out to the reservation and look there."

"I hate to think what the Indians would do to them. They might turn them into slaves."

"Hiram, the Indians haven't kidnapped children around here for twenty years. They would have no use for our kids."

"I can't breathe," Mr. Walker said.

"Pete, can you get Mr. Walker a glass of water," the sheriff said.

I ran over to the container of water next to the stove. I scooped out some water and poured it into a metal cup. I walked over and handed it to Abby's dad.

"Thank you, son."

"Okay, Hiram, I want you to think. When's the last time you saw them?"

"They were out working in the fields this morning, but

they never came back for lunch. It's not like them to miss a meal, so I went out to look for them. I searched for a couple of hours but couldn't find them. That's when I decided to come here."

"Do you have any kin in the area?" the sheriff asked. "Could they have gone there?"

"The only kin we have in the state is Martha's cousin, but she lives in Kansas City. That's a hundred and fifty miles. There's no way they could have gotten there on their own."

"Pete, you can jump in here any time you want," the sheriff said.

I hesitated at first, and then decided to join the conversation. "Mr. Walker, do you know what they were wearing when they left the house?"

The sheriff winked at me. I had asked the right question.

"Tommy was wearing a short-sleeve...collared...button-up...white shirt...with brown pants. I remember 'cause I asked him why he was wearin' a Sunday School shirt to work the fields. And he said 'cause all his other shirts were dirty."

"And how about Abby?" I said.

He thought for a moment. "She had on a blue dress that went down to her ankles and a blue bonnet."

"Good, good," the sheriff said. "That's gonna help."

"Can I ask another question, Sheriff?" I said.

"Pete, you're doin' great. Ask as many as you like."

"Okay." I turned to Mr. Walker. "Does Abby have any friends from school who live in the area?"

"Yeah, she does."

"Is it possible she went to visit one of them and lost track of the time?" I asked.

"I don't know. Maybe."

I ran over to the sheriff's desk, opened a drawer, and pulled out a piece of paper and a pencil. I brought them over to Mr. Walker.

"Here, can you jot down the names of Abby's friends. And maybe you could include Tommy's friends while you're at it."

The sheriff smiled at me and nodded. I could tell he approved. We waited while Mr. Walker wrote down the names of his children's friends.

"And how about Abby's or Tommy's school teachers?" I said.

Mr. Walker scribbled down a couple more names on the paper.

"Can I ask if Abby or Tommy has ever run away from home before," I said.

"No, never."

"Have they ever gone off by themselves when they were mad about something?"

"Yeah, a couple of times. Whenever they get moody, they head down to the stream and sit under a black walnut tree."

"I assume you looked there?" I said.

"Yeah, it was one of the first places I checked."

"Do you know if they were carrying anything with them? Toy? Water jug? Anything?"

He thought for a moment. "As a matter of fact, Abby was carrying her favorite doll, Matilda. It's small—only about seven or eight inches tall. She's wearing a red-and-white polka dot dress, and she has long blond hair. Whenever Abby was working, she would slide the doll inside the belt around her waist."

"Did you happen to find that doll while you were looking for them?"

"No, I didn't see it. And I would have remembered it if I had seen it."

"Okay, thanks. Sheriff, that's all I have."

"Hiram," the sheriff said, "is there anything else you can think of that'll help us find your children?"

"Nothing comes to mind." He dropped his head. "I don't think I could go on living if anything happened to either one of them."

"Don't talk like that," the sheriff said. "We're gonna find them. I promise."

I was wondering how smart it was for the sheriff to say something like that. I didn't think today's law enforcement officers ever made those kinds of promises. But I knew the sheriff's comment was straight from the heart. He would do anything in his power to bring back those kids alive and healthy.

"All right, Hiram, I want you to go home and take care of your wife. Leave this in our hands. Try to think positive thoughts, okay?"

"I'll try." Abby's father stood dejectedly. His shoulders slumped. He looked defeated. It was hard to imagine what he was feeling at that moment. He nodded and walked out the door.

"Okay, Pete, hand me that list of friends. We'll plot out our next moves."

I picked up the paper and stared at a list of about ten names. I handed it to the sheriff.

"Do you recognize any of these families?" I said.

The sheriff studied the names. "I know all of them. And I know exactly where their houses or farms or ranches are. A couple of them live in town. We'll start there." He walked over to his desk and fumbled for something in the top drawer. He eventually pulled out a map of the area. "Okay here we are." He pointed to the town of Abilene. Then he began placing X's on various locations. Under each one, he printed the name of a family. Then he drew an arrow from Abilene to the first X, and then another arrow to the next X, and so on. "Pete, run over to the livery stable and ask Jeremiah to saddle up our horses."

I grabbed my hat and ran out the door. I hustled down to the livery stable. When I got there, Jeremiah was brushing one of the horses. I was out of breath.

"Mr. Adams, can you saddle up my horse and the sheriff's as soon as you have a chance."

"Relax, Pete. What's the rush?"

I wasn't sure if I should say anything, but then I figured the more people who knew about it, the better chance we had of finding those kids.

"Abby Walker and her brother have gone missing. Her parents can't find them anywhere. The sheriff and I are gonna go look for them."

"Oh, dear," he said. "That's awful." He looked out a window toward the open plains. "It's not safe for children to be out there alone. Bad things can happen. I'll get those horses saddled up right away. And I'll keep my eyes open for those youngin's."

"Thanks a lot," I said. "We'll be back in a few minutes." Jeremiah waved as I ran off. I made it back to the office in a couple of minutes. The sheriff was busy packing up some grub for the ride. He grabbed a bedroll from a shelf and tossed it to me. "You'll be needing this. We might not be back for a couple of days." He opened the door and looked out. "Those are rain clouds. You'd better pack a change of clothes." He pointed to a cabinet. There's a couple of rain slicks in there. You'll wanna pack 'em too. We may need them if it comes down really hard.

I had never been out on the prairie in a driving rainstorm before. This was going to be a new experience. When there was nowhere to take cover, it was just you versus Mother Nature, and I'll bet she usually won. We spent the next few minutes packing up last-minute items. There was just so much you could take on horseback. Once it seemed we were ready to go, the sheriff motioned for me to join him at his desk.

He pulled out the map. "We're right here," he said, pointing to an X. "On our way out of town, we're gonna stop at the Thompson house. Joshua Thompson is a bookkeeper here. He has a daughter, Margaret, who goes to school with Abby." He pointed to another X on the map. "Then we'll stop at the Chatsworth house. Their daughter, Grace, is another one of Abby's friends. Then we'll head out to the Walker farm. We'll see if we can find any hoof prints or wheel tracks near where the children were working. Hopefully we can find some and they'll lead us to them." He glanced out the window. "We'd better hurry. The rain'll be here soon. It'll wash away the tracks if we're too late."

And, so, my first real Old West adventure had begun. I was excited about the prospect of accompanying the sheriff in a missing persons' case. But I was also troubled by the fact that Abby was the one missing. I tried not to think about what might have happened to her. It was just too painful. I felt bad for Tommy as well. He was just a little guy. He had to be really scared. The more I thought about the whole thing, the angrier I became. Who was mean or sick or deranged enough to kidnap children? It had to be a monster of some kind. I only hoped that we weren't too late. I shook my head. I had to stop thinking like that. I needed to be more positive. We were going to find them safe and sound. And things would end happily ever after. At least, I hoped they would.

CHAPTER 10

OUR FIRST STOP WAS MARGARET THOMPSON'S HOUSE. SHE went to school with Abby. We rode up to a large house on the outskirts of town. It was a stone building with tall columns in front. There were several flower boxes filled with red petunias. An iron fence surrounded the property. We got down from our horses and tied them to the fence.

"Pretty nice place, huh?" the sheriff said.

I nodded. We opened the gate and walked up to the front door. There was a rope dangling in front of us. The sheriff pulled it. We could hear bells ringing from inside. A moment later, a woman answered the door.

"Oh, hello, Sheriff. Can I help you?" she said. She was wearing a long, flowing green dress with yellow flowers on it.

"Kate, sorry to bother you, but I'd like to speak with Margaret."

"Margaret? Has she done anything wrong?"

"No, nothing like that." The sheriff hesitated. "I understand that she's a friend of Abby Walker. Is that correct?"

"Yes, they're close friends."

"Abby and her brother, Tommy...are missing."

Mrs. Thompson covered her mouth with her hands. "How horrid! Do you have any idea what happened?"

"I'm afraid not. We're just starting our investigation," he said. "We'd just like to know if Margaret has seen Abby lately. We're checking with all her friends."

"Of course. Come right in," she said. "Please wait right here. I'll get Margaret."

We stood in the entryway quietly for a minute before a young girl about my age appeared. She was wearing a long white dress tied at the waist. I couldn't believe how girls dressed in the Old West. It was so formal. Did they play in these clothes too, I wondered?

"Hello, Sheriff," she said, "can I be of help?"

"Hi, Margaret, how are you?"

"I'm fine, sir."

"Margaret, have you seen Abby Walker lately?"

Margaret thought to herself for a moment. "I saw her two days ago. My mother had baked a rhubarb pie that morning, so we went over to the Walker farm with it."

"What did you and Abby talk about?"

She blushed and shrugged. "You know, Sheriff. Girl stuff."

The sheriff and I both smiled. "By the way, dear, this is my assistant, Pete."

"How do you do, Pete?" she said.

"Do you recall if Abby said anything about going anywhere or doing anything," the sheriff asked.

"She complained a little about having to pull weeds in the fields in this heat."

"But nothing else?"

"No, I'm sorry," she said.

I decided it was my turn to join the interrogation.

"Margaret, can you think of anyone who might want to harm her?"

"Abby? Oh, goodness, no. Everyone likes her."

"Have any boys shown an interest in her?" I asked.

She started to blush again. "Well, sure. Abby's very popular. There are some boys who like her."

"Can you tell me their names?"

"Let me think. There's Henry Anderson...Dwight Booker...and...Fred Kimball."

"Any of them the jealous types?"

"Fred Kimball. He asked Abby to a dance one time but she said no. Then he told Henry and Dwight that if either of them asked her, they'd be sorry."

"And nothing ever came of it?"

"If you ask me...Fred's all talk."

I extended my hand to shake. "Well, thank you. You've been very helpful." I looked over my shoulder at the sheriff who was smiling with his arms folded."

He leaned over and whispered to me. "I don't know what I'm doing here. You don't need my help." He waved to Margaret's mom in the next room. "Thanks, Kate. We'll be on our way."

She walked us to the door. "I surely hope you find those children. It makes me sick to think of them in harm's way."

"If you hear of anything that might be helpful, you'll let us know?"

"Of course."

We walked out onto the front porch and headed back to the horses.

"Fred Kimball, huh?"

"What about him?" I said.

"I had a run-in with that youngin' a few months back. I wouldn't put anything past him."

"What did he do?"

"His dad, who's as bad as he is, bought him a new Winchester rifle—the repeating rifle—for his birthday."

"*Repeating*?" I asked.

"It allows you to fire a number of shots without having to reload. So, young Mr. Kimball decided to rid the territory of cats and dogs. These were peoples' pets. He'd sit in the brush and pick off helpless animals. When I caught him, I was so angry, I threw him in jail. I threw a twelve-year-old in jail. It didn't stick as you might guess."

"So, what happened to him?"

"When the traveling judge came through, we had a trial. The judge told him he couldn't touch another rifle till his eighteenth birthday. And he made the young man's father pay restitution to all of the families whose pets he had killed."

"Did he pay?" I asked.

"He refused to at first, but when I threatened to throw his sorry butt in jail if he didn't, he eventually paid up."

"So, what do you think, Sheriff. Is this kid messed up enough to kidnap a fellow classmate and her little brother?"

"To tell you the truth, I don't know. But we're gonna have to go out there and talk to them. It's a day's ride, so we'll put that visit off till we've spoken to the others." He stopped to think to himself for a moment. "When you went out to the Walker farm with Doc, did you notice their dog, Killer?"

"Sure," I said. "The three-legged dog."

"And do you know why he's missing a leg? Think real hard."

I knew I should probably know the answer, but I was struggling. Then, all at once, I had it.

"Fred Kimball?"

The sheriff nodded. "One of his shots shattered Killer's right front leg. There was no way to save it, so they had to take it off. But, at least, he survived."

"What a rat!" I said.

"That's one way to describe him," the sheriff said. He pulled the map from his pocket and unfolded it. "Let's see. Our next stop is Wilma Chatsworth's. She's a seamstress in town. She's got a place about two hundred yards that way." He pointed. "Her daughter, Grace, is on the list of Abby's friends that Hiram gave us."

We hopped on our horses and headed in the opposite direction.

"Sheriff, I never asked you—does your horse have a name? I mean, my horse."

"I call her Shuffle."

"Shuffle? Why?

"You may not have noticed but after you hit the sack at night, I wander over to the Ranchview Saloon and play a little poker. It's how I wind down each day. And since I'm a pretty fair hand at shuffling the cards, it's just seemed like a good name."

I reached over and petted Shuffle's mane. "Then Shuffle, it is." We headed across town to speak with Grace Chatsworth. The clouds were building. And they were dark. I was pretty certain we'd be wearing those rain slicks before long. It only took a couple of minutes to reach Grace's house. This one was unlike the last one. The house was definitely in need of repair. The shutters were hanging by a thread. Two of the windows were broken. Paint was peeling. Half of the fence in the front yard had fallen over. We tied our horses up to part of the fence still standing and walked up to the front door. Before the sheriff could knock, the door opened. A young girl with a killer smile greeted us.

"Hi, Sheriff Malone. What are you doing here?"

"Hello, Grace," he said. "My, that's a pretty dress you're wearing."

"Thank you. My momma made it."

"Your momma is the finest seamstress in all of Abilene."

Grace smiled. "Do you want me to get her for you?"

"Actually, we came here to see you."

"Me? Really?"

The sheriff nodded.

"Would you like to come in?" she said.

"Just for a couple of minutes maybe."

I couldn't help but notice that the inside of the house was in the same condition as the outside. A couple of the walls were in desperate need of a paint job. And the rug on the floor was tattered and full of holes.

"Would you like to sit down?" Grace said.

"No, we won't be here that long," the sheriff answered. "Listen, Grace, you're friends with Abby Walker, right?"

"Uh-huh."

"Have you seen Abby lately?"

Grace put her finger to her lips. "Not in about a week, I guess. I bumped into her in town."

"Did you talk about anything?"

The entire time, Grace seemed to be sneaking a peek at me. I kind of liked the attention.

"Not really. It was more like 'Hi,' 'How are you?' 'We should get together soon.' Stuff like that."

The sheriff noticed the next time Grace stared at me.

"Now, where are my manners? Miss Grace Chatsworth, meet my apprentice, Mr. Pete Moss."

"*Pete Moss*, did you say?"

"Yeah, it's kind of a funny name," I said.

"No, it's a nice name." She smiled. "Easy to remember."

"Pete, have I left anything out?" the sheriff said.

"I do have a question. Grace, do you and Abby have any kind of a secret hiding place where you would go when you don't want anyone to find you?"

She grinned. "Well, there is this place. It's an old, abandoned cabin near the mouth of the river."

"The old Dickerson place?" the sheriff asked.

She nodded.

"Add that to our list, Pete," the sheriff said.

"Okay."

"Sheriff, has something happened to Abby?" Grace said.

"Well, yes, Abby and her brother have gone missing, and we're desperately trying to find them."

Grace tensed up. The color left her face. "Oh, no, that's terrible. Do you think they're okay?"

"I sure hope so," the sheriff said. "We're doing everything we can to locate them. If you think of anything that might help us, will you come and tell me?"

"I sure will. I'd do anything for Abby."

"I know you would," the sheriff said. "Well, we'd better get going. You tell your momma we were here, okay?"

"I will."

The sheriff put his hand on her head and smiled. We left and walked out. "Nice people," he said.

"Is Grace's dad around?" I asked.

"No. And they're better off without him. He was a

bum. He gambled away every penny they earned. He walked out on them two years ago. But Wilma has done a great job making ends meet and raising a fine daughter." He looked out toward the prairie, then up at the clouds. "We'd better head out to the Walker farm before the rain comes. We need to check for any tracks that our kidnappers might have left behind."

The winds started to pick up as we crossed the prairie. The dust was blowing in our faces. The sheriff suggested we pull our kerchiefs up over our nose and mouth. I couldn't help but think we might have looked like a couple of bandits with our faces covered. But the shiny star on the sheriff's chest was all people needed to see to know we were the good guys.

The further away from town we traveled, the darker the clouds got. We were a couple of miles out of Abilene when we felt the first drops. Within minutes, the skies opened up. The sheriff motioned for us to stop under a tree about a hundred yards in front of us. When we got there, we pulled our rain slicks out and slipped them on. They were like big, clear, plastic ponchos. They didn't cover our heads. That's what our hats were for. We soon took off again in the direction of the Walker farm. It poured the entire way. When we finally got there, we tied up the horses and ran to the front door and knocked.

"Are we just gonna leave the horses out in the rain?" I asked.

The sheriff smiled. "They'll be just fine."

Before we could even knock, Hiram Walker was standing in the doorway. "Hello, Sheriff, have you got any news for us?"

"Not yet, but we just started our investigation. I'm sure we'll turn up something soon."

"Please come in," he said.

Killer immediately came up to greet us. He was kind of standoffish at first but when I crouched down to pet him, he licked my hand. We were officially buddies.

"Hiram, I need you to take me to the spot in the fields where the children were last working. Can you do that?"

"Certainly. Let me tell Martha we're headed out for a bit." He disappeared into an adjoining room. A moment later, a woman in a nightgown and robe appeared. Her hair was a mess. She looked pale.

"Thank you for coming out, Sheriff," she said. Her voice was weak. It cracked.

"Martha, there was no need for you to get up," the sheriff said. "Please go back to bed."

"I will. You'll help us find our youngin's, won't you? Please."

"I'll do everything I can. Now you go lie down."

She nodded and disappeared into the bedroom.

"I'm going to take the buckboard out there," Mr. Walker said. "You wanna follow me?"

The sheriff nodded.

We followed Mr. Walker out of the house. He walked into the barn, and a minute later he returned, now behind the reins of a buckboard. He tossed us a couple of rags which we used to dry off our saddles. He soon headed out and we followed. The rain had let up a bit but was still coming down. We traveled about a mile down a narrow dirt road when Mr. Walker pulled over and stopped. He pointed into one of the fields.

"They were about fifty yards in that direction when I last saw them," he said.

The sheriff got off his horse and studied the ground. He crouched down and picked up a handful of dirt which had now turned to mud. He looked up at the skies and frowned.

"The rain has washed out any tracks that might have been here."

Mr. Walker dropped his head. "We're never gonna find them, are we, Sheriff?"

"Now don't say that. It's early. We have a lot of places to check. A lot of people to talk to. It's very possible that someone saw something. Just go back home and tend to your wife. Leave this to us."

Mr. Walker nodded. He turned the buckboard around and headed back to the farm. The rain had just about stopped. The sheriff got back up onto his horse and sighed.

"What's wrong?" I said.

"*What's wrong? Everything's wrong.* The Walker children have vanished. And we have no clues, no suspects, no evidence, and no way of tracking who might have taken them. The longer they're missing, the greater the chance we won't find them alive. Other than that, everything is just fine," he said sarcastically.

It was then that I started to think that we might never find these kids. I had always believed they would show up and we'd be able to return them home to their parents. But the look on the sheriff's face said everything. He was discouraged. He was defeated. And I was fearful that this might change from a rescue mission to a recovery effort.

CHAPTER 11

WE VISITED A COUPLE MORE RANCHES IN THE AREA WHERE some of Abby's friends lived. Neither stop panned out. The girls we had spoken to hadn't seen Abby since school had let out for the summer some six weeks earlier. But one thing was curious. When we brought up the name of Fred Kimball, both girls made faces. Neither of them was a fan of young Mr. Kimball. They told us how he bullied weaker kids at school and talked back to the teachers on a regular basis. The more I learned about this character, the less I liked him, and the more I wanted to avoid him. But that was not an option. We would have to eventually confront him. I just hoped the sheriff was at my side when that occurred.

The last family we visited before dark kindly offered us shelter for the night. They had six kids of their own so the only place to bunk down was in the barn. It smelled awful but the hay was a heck of a lot drier and softer than the wet, hard grounds on the prairie. The sheriff sat with his back against one of the bales while chewing a piece o f hay. I could tell he was deep in thought. He wanted to crack this case so badly. And it wasn't because he'd be viewed as some kind of hero, but rather to bring relief to Mr. and Mrs. Walker. I knew from my research that Amos Malone had never married and never had children of his own. But you could tell he would have made a great dad. He knew how to talk to kids. He knew how to relate to them. And I was living proof of that. He never made me feel like I was in the way. He allowed me to participate in his world, including the interrogation of witnesses.

I drifted off a few minutes later. When I awoke the next morning, I jumped out of my skin, thanks to a rooster who positioned himself only a few feet away. It was five thirty and time to rise and shine if you lived on a farm. The lady of the house surprised us with eggs over-easy and a stack of flapjacks. It was a great breakfast and a perfect way to start the day. Once we were done exchanging pleasantries with the homeowners, we were off again. The sun was out, and the skies were clear. It looked as if we wouldn't be dodging raindrops this day. When we were a couple of miles out, the sheriff pulled over and stopped.

"Let's get that map out and plot our course for the day," he said.

I jumped down from my horse and dug the map out of the sheriff's saddlebag. "We can eliminate these places." I pointed to four X's on the map. "How about if we head to—"

"Wait a second, Pete. You know what I'd like to do?"

I shook my head.

"I'd like to check out that old, abandoned Dickerson shack—the one Grace talked about. It might be a waste of time, but I'd feel better if we could cross that off our list."

"Sounds good to me."

"Let's do that then."

Since it had cleared up, we packed up our rain slicks. I hopped back on old Shuffle and we headed north. The sheriff was quiet during the ride. I could tell he was thinking about something. I wondered if this might be a good time to warn him about the fateful card game on July 11th—the one that would be his last—unless I did something about it. Two and a half weeks had passed since I had blown away the dust from *The Man Who Tamed the Wild West. The Unauthorized Biography of Amos "Lone Wolf" Malone* by Don Kent, and returned back to Abilene, Kansas, in 1888. I had twelve days left to try to make the sheriff listen to me about his future. I had respected his wishes about not doing anything that might change the course of future events, but I was determined to keep Amos Malone alive and well for years to come. Although I wanted to find Abby and Tommy as soon as possible, I was actually hoping we would still be in the midst of this search and rescue effort so that he wouldn't have time to play poker on the night of July 11th.

"Hey, Sheriff," I said. "I don't suppose you've changed your mind about letting me warn you about the future."

"Not in the slightest."

"But it's something that you really need to know."

"Pete, have you forgotten what I told you? If you tell me, and if I end up avoiding something that was meant to be, then it won't just change my life, it will change history as we know it, and affect the lives of hundreds, maybe thousands, of other people. I appreciate your concern, but it's best this way."

I kind of understood what he was saying but my main concern was saving this man's life, and I was determined to do it. Whether he would take my advice was still up in the air, but when the time was right, I would reveal to him where and how he was to take his last breath. He could then decide if he was willing to change his mind. I truly believed when he thought about how to avoid an unplanned trip to Boot Hill, he would listen to me and do everything in his power to come out of this alive.

We rode on for the next hour. It wasn't long before we came upon a river. We stopped to water the horses before continuing on. I remembered that Grace had said this old shack was near the mouth of the river, so I was hoping we were getting close. The rain had helped keep the dust down. It wasn't blowing in our faces the way it had the day before. Every so often, we'd pass an animal carcass. There were all kinds—rabbits, prairie dogs, buffalo, cattle, and an occasional mountain lion.

"How much farther?" I asked.

"It's right over that ridge," he said.

And minutes later, I could see the roof of a shack. Soon the entire structure was visible. There wasn't much to it. All of the windows were broken. The shutters were hanging off. It needed a new coat of paint in the worst way. The roof had holes in it. It didn't look like a very safe place for kids to play. We rode right up to it and got down off our horses. We tied them to a small tree in the front yard. The sheriff walked up to a door which was half open. He knocked, never expecting to find any occupants. When we heard a moan coming from inside, we entered the shack. It was really dark inside. It took a few moments for our eyes to adjust. Then we spotted him.

"Oh, no," the sheriff uttered.

We walked over to a boy, no more than fourteen or fifteen, lying in the corner of the shack. It was obvious by the way he was dressed that he was Native American. He was badly hurt. His right eye was swollen shut. His bottom lip was puffy. There was blood coming from his forehead.

"He's Cheyenne," the sheriff said.

"What happened to him do you think?"

"That's what I'm going to try to find out." The sheriff bent down and reached out his hand. The boy pulled away and covered up. He was clearly afraid. "I'm not going to hurt you," the sheriff said. "He doesn't appear to speak English. My Cheyenne is a little rusty but I'm going to give it a try." A strange series of sounds came from the sheriff's lips.

I couldn't tell what any of it meant.

The boy turned toward him. His eyes seemed to recognize that this person meant him no harm. He spoke a few words. Then for the next couple of minutes, the two of them spoke non-stop. The boy tried to sit up. The sheriff helped him.

"He's Cheyenne, all right. He got lost. He drifted off the reservation and ended up near a herd of buffalo. And then two buffalo hunters spotted him. They chased him to this shack and beat him within an inch of his life."

"Could those be the same two that came into the office that day?"

"Gotta be," the sheriff said. "Listen, Pete, there's been a change of plans. I'm going to ride into town and bring Doc Conrad out here. This boy's too weak to ride back with us. Then I'm going to head out to try and find those buffalo hunters."

"What should I do?" I asked. "Should I wait here with him?"

"No. There's not much you can do for him right now. I want you to continue to question Abby's and Tommy's friends. We have to find those children, and it's gotta be our top priority. But I can't very well ignore this boy and leave him here to die. We need to split up and work on both cases at the same time. Can you do that? Can you continue on alone?"

"Sure," I said. But I really wasn't. First of all, even with a map, I wasn't certain of my way around this territory. And second, would these families allow me, a total stranger, a kid no less, to talk to their children? I wasn't sure they would, but I would soon find out. I totally agreed with the sheriff that finding Abby and Tommy was our number one concern. And we couldn't waste precious time. Every minute that passed could be the difference between life and death.

"Would you go out there and get my canteen," the sheriff said. "I'm going to leave it with the boy while I'm gone."

I ran outside and retrieved it for him. "You'd better take a major swig to hold you," I said.

"Now you're thinking." The sheriff took a long drink. Then he lifted the injured boy's head and poured some water into his mouth. "Pete, would you mind getting the map for me. I want to show you where we are."

I headed out and fumbled through the sheriff's saddle bags until I located the map. I unfolded it and headed back into the shack.

"Here," I said as I handed it to him.

He knelt down and flattened the map out on the dirt floor. "Okay, here's the river. And right over here is where we are. You got that?"

I nodded.

"All right, it might make sense for you to visit the Morrells first." He pointed to an X on the map. "That's where one of Tommy's friends lives. Then head south about three miles and talk to the Ketchams." He pointed to another X. "Their daughter goes to school with Abby. Then go northeast to the Sampson ranch. They have a son and daughter who both know the missing children. Then I think you oughta head back to town. I don't want you camping out by yourself tonight. I might be at the office, or I might not be. It all depends on if Doc and I can get the boy back into town, and how soon I need to leave to catch those buffalo hunters."

The sheriff seemed to have a lot of confidence in me. I only wished I felt the same way about myself. He seemed to think I could continue questioning Abby's and Tommy's friends without a problem. I couldn't let him know I was scared—really scared. Scared to be alone out on the prairie. Scared to be traveling in unknown waters. Scared to go up to complete strangers and ask to talk to their kids. I wanted to stay with the sheriff in the worst way. I wished I could accompany him back to town to get Doc Conrad. I would have liked nothing better than to ride back to the shack with both of them so Doc could care for the injured boy. We were a team, right? At least, we had been up until now. Why break that up?

And then I stopped to think about what I had been saying. I felt bad—really bad. I was being completely self-ish. I was more concerned about my own safety than that of Abby and Tommy. I had accepted this assignment with the knowledge that some tasks might be more difficult than others. Here now was a chance to show my stuff. It was a chance to show the sheriff that he hadn't made a mistake by plucking me out of the library basement. Of all the people he could have chosen to be his successor, he had picked me. I owed him more than this. What would he think of me if he knew I had been whining about doing my job? He would have known that he had made a poor choice. I couldn't let him down. I had to handle this task courageously and show him he had made not only the right decision, but the perfect decision.

I folded up the map and slid it into my front shirt pocket. "I'd better be on my way," I said.

"I feel bad leaving you out here with no way of defending yourself," the sheriff said. "Maybe I should leave you my rifle."

As exciting as that sounded, I knew it was a mistake. "That's okay, sheriff. I've never fired a gun before. I'd probably manage to hurt myself with it. I'll be fine. Don't worry."

"All right, but if you get into any trouble, you jump on Shuffle and you ride hard and fast back to Abilene. You hear me?"

"I got it." I climbed up onto my horse, took a minute to figure out the direction I should be heading, waved goodbye to the sheriff, and was on my way. I looked left, right, in front of me, and behind me as I rode. I wanted to be ready for any surprises. I had a job to do, and I wasn't going to let my nerves get the better of me. I was determined to find Abby and Tommy, and I would go to any means necessary to secure their safety. I wouldn't hesitate to put my own life on the line to make that happen. After all, I was Pete Moss, the apprentice to Sheriff Amos *Lone Wolf* Malone. I was relentless. I was unstoppable. I was fearless. At least, I hoped I was.

CHAPTER 12

I HAD RIDDEN ABOUT FIFTEEN MINUTES WITHOUT SEEING A single person. And I was perfectly fine with that. It wasn't that I enjoyed being alone, I just wasn't sure what kinds of characters might be lurking out here. After all, this was the Old West. Lawlessness ran rampant. At least it did in all the westerns I had ever read. If there wasn't a sheriff or marshal close by, some people did whatever they wanted, and they never looked back. They had no respect for the law. They followed what they liked to call *frontier justice*. They didn't wait around for a lawman or a judge to settle their disputes. They created their own laws. I sure as heck didn't want to bump into one of those folks.

I pulled the map from my pocket and took a close look at my first stop—the Sam Morrell farm. I wanted to make sure I was still on the right course. The sheriff had written the name of Micah Morrell under the X. He had to be one of Tommy's friends. I looked around to get a sense of where I was on the map, and then took a second look at where the Morrell farm was. It appeared I would need to ride north-northeast. I pointed Shuffle in that direction and continued on my way. I started walking her, but that soon increased to a trot. I would keep her at that pace for as long as she was able. I looked around. There was nothing but prairie as far as the eye could see. The grass was green and brown and flat. I kept my eyes on the terrain. I didn't want Shuffle to step into any holes. If she came up lame, we'd both be in trouble.

I rode a few more miles, and then in the distance, I saw a white farmhouse and a red barn. Hopefully, I had stumbled onto the Morrell farm. I traveled a few more minutes on a bumpy dirt trail. It led me right up to the house. I stopped and looked around. I didn't see anyone. And then a woman, fixing her hair and wearing a white apron, stepped out of the house and started walking toward me.

"Can I help you, young man?"

I got down off my horse. "Excuse me, my name is Pete Moss."

She looked at me rather strangely. Her reaction was the same as most people I had met since I'd gotten here. I probably should have picked a different name. Every time people heard *Pete Moss*, they did a double-take. What kind of a name is that, they must have thought. But it was too late now to change it. I was stuck with it.

"I'm working with Sheriff Malone. We're investigating a missing persons' case."

"Why did he send you?" the woman said. "Why didn't he come here himself?"

I should have been prepared for that. "He got called away on a more important matter. He asked me to handle this for him."

"Who's missing?" the woman said. She looked at me

with disapproval. She wasn't buying this sheriff's helper business.

"Abigail and Tommy Walker," I said. "No one's seen them since yesterday afternoon."

The woman's expression changed. She seemed concerned. "Abby and Tommy?"

"Yes. And I was wondering if I might speak with Micah. I understand he's one of Tommy's friends. I'd like to know the last time he saw him. He might be able to help."

She looked back at the house. "Of course. I'll fetch him."

A minute or so later, the woman reappeared. She was holding her son by the hand.

"Micah, this young man has a few questions for you. I want you to answer him truthfully."

"Yes, Mother," the boy said.

I wondered if the boy was prone to fibbing. That would explain his mother's directions. For the next several minutes, I asked Micah a prepared list of questions regarding the disappearance. He seemed thoughtful and honest in his responses. But by the end of the interview, I wasn't any closer to finding the missing kids. Micah hadn't shed any new light on things. I was beginning to wonder if interviewing friends was the best strategy. The only piece of useful information we had discovered yet was the role that Fred Kimball may have played. And that was a long-shot at best. There was no evidence linking Fred to the missing kids. The fact that he was a bully and a trouble-maker was all we had to go on.

Next stop was the Ketcham farm about three miles due south. I pointed Shuffle in that direction and was on my way. I could tell by the position of the sun that it was about two or three in the afternoon. I reached into my saddlebags and grabbed a stale muffin the sheriff had packed for me. Since it was the only thing I had had to eat since breakfast, I didn't even notice how hard and crumbly it was. I washed it down with a swig of water. Unlike earlier, there were more people on the trails this time. I came upon an old man in a buckboard who nodded at me as we passed. He seemed pretty harmless. Then I encountered a well-dressed couple in a covered buggy. I tried to make eye contact with them, but they looked away at the last minute. They were either unfriendly or fearful of strangers. I didn't take it personally.

Within a few minutes, I spotted a set of buildings in the distance. There was a farmhouse, a barn, a silo and a couple of smaller shacks. This farm had to be a larger operation, I thought. I pulled the map from my pocket. It had the name *Sarah* under the X. It had to be one of Abby's friends. The path that led up to the Ketcham farm was flat and clean. No holes. No boulders. It was easier on Shuffle. I was glad. I could see two or three men working the fields. I rode past them right up to the farmhouse. There was some livestock in pens next to the barn—a few cows, some sheep, and something that looked like a bull. I kept my distance from him. I hopped off my horse and just stood there for a few moments. I was hoping someone would notice me. I wasn't particularly comfortable just walking up to the front door of the farmhouse and knocking. Within a few seconds, a man emerged from the barn. He looked up and walked over.

"Can I help you, stranger?" he asked.

I walked over and extended my hand. "Good afternoon, sir. Is your name Mr. Ketcham?"

He smiled cautiously. "Moses Ketcham, yes."

"Well, my name is Pete Moss." I decided to quickly rattle off my reason for being there so he didn't have time to think about how odd my name must have sounded. "I'm working with Sheriff Malone. We're investigating the disappearance of two of your neighbors."

"And who would that be?"

"Abigail and Tommy Walker."

"Heavens! They're missing?"

"Yeah, since about this time yesterday."

"Do you have any idea where they might be?"

"Not really," I said. "We're just trying to talk to some of Abby's and Tommy's friends to see if they remember seeing them. I understand your daughter, Sarah, is a friend of Abby's. Do you think it would it be possible for me to speak to her?"

"Of course." Mr. Ketcham turned toward the house and yelled out. "Sarah! Come out here."

Moments later, a girl in a short-sleeve yellow shirt and riding pants appeared. "Yes, Papa."

"Sarah, a terrible thing has happened. This young man needs your help."

"What is it?" she asked.

"Someone may have kidnapped Abby and Tommy Walker," her dad said. "They're missing and no one can seem to find them."

"Oh, dear," she said. She covered her mouth with both hands. "How terrible! What can I do?"

Mr. Ketcham nodded at me. And so, I began yet another interview. I asked her all of the questions I had asked the others, plus a few more I thought up at the last minute. But by the end of my interrogation, I was no closer to solving the case. I thanked Sarah and her father for their time and was on my way. I was getting frustrated. Each of these interviews took time—precious time—and every minute that passed was another minute Abby and Tommy were spending with their captor. And who knew if they were being mistreated or not. Whenever I tried to imagine what had happened to them, I pictured myself saving them single-handedly and beating the snot out of the monster who had taken them. But considering the fact that I had never been the most physical person out there, it was unlikely I would use fisticuffs to settle this dispute.

Even though there didn't appear to be much sun left in the day, I decided I needed to try to visit one more family before heading back into town. The map indicated that next on the list was the Sampson ranch. I pointed Shuffle northeast and we were off. I was starting to get a little worried about riding back into town at night, but I figured that was still safer than camping out on the prairie alone. Who knew what sort of dangers I might encounter by doing so? I rode hard and fast to my final destination. Within a few miles, I came upon a fresh stream. This was perfect. It was a chance for Shuffle to quench her thirst. I was surprised how long she stopped to drink. But I didn't rush her. She had been a faithful partner through it all, and I didn't want to do anything that might harm her.

I reached the Sampson ranch about twenty minutes later. This was a big spread. There was a fence that seemed to go on forever, and inside were some of the most beautiful horses I had ever seen. There were black ones, white ones, and even an Appaloosa. Then there was another section of fencing with cattle—dozens of them. This place was no mom and pop operation, that was for sure. There was some definite money here. I rode up to a huge white farmhouse, stopped Shuffle, and jumped off. I tied her up to a hitching post nearby. I looked around for any signs of life. I was soon met by a large, angry rancher.

"Who are you?" the man said. He wore a checkered shirt and large black hat. He was holding a shotgun.

"Excuse me, sir. My name is Pete Moss. I'm working with Sheriff Malone. We're investigating the disappearance of two children in the area. And I was wondering if I might speak to your son and daughter. I think they're friends of the missing children."

"You're not talking to my kids. Get off this ranch."

"I promise I wouldn't take more than a couple of minutes. It's just that we're trying to talk to as many people as possible who may have seen the kids before they disappeared."

He cocked the shotgun. "You say you're working with Amos Malone?"

"Yes."

"Well, that's reason enough to drive you off this ranch. I don't particularly cotton to the law tellin' me what I can and can't do. So, you get back on that horse and ride. And don't look back."

I noticed a boy about Tommy's age sticking his head out of the barn door. I needed to talk to that kid in the worst way, but I didn't want to risk my life doing so. My instincts were telling me to jump on Shuffle and get as far away from this ranch as possible. But what if this rancher's kids had important information that might help us find Abby and Tommy? If I didn't find that out, and something terrible happened to those kids, I would never forgive myself.

"So, sir, as I was saying—"

"By the way, if you're working for the sheriff, where's your badge, *lawman*?"

That was a great question. Why *didn't* I have a badge? How could the sheriff expect me to walk up to complete strangers and have them believe I worked for him? I would have to discuss this matter with him later. I wasn't sure if an apprentice was allowed to wear a badge, but would it kill him to give me one that said *deputy* or something. It would give me a little credibility with some of these folks.

"Well...I'll have to ask him...but I'm definitely working for the sheriff."

"I don't care if you're working for the president. Get back on that horse and get off my land."

I just stood there. I wasn't sure how to respond.

"You got a hearing problem, son?"

"No, I'm leaving." I looked back at the barn. Mr. Sampson's son was still spying on us. I needed to figure out a way to talk to him. Who knows? This kid could be the missing link. Every piece of information was crucial to this case. I climbed aboard Shuffle, turned him in the direction of the exit, and began my retreat. Every few seconds, I'd look over my shoulder to see if Mr. Sampson or his son was still watching me. When I had passed all of the cattle and horses, and reached the main gate, I stopped. I decided I wasn't leaving until I had spoken to that little boy. I took a look at the map. The sheriff had written down *Susan* and *Theodore* under the X marking the Sampson ranch. Okay, so now I knew their names. Now all I had to do was get back on that property without being seen. It wasn't going to be easy. And it wasn't going to be safe. I had no interest in getting reacquainted with that shotgun.

I continued to study the map. I noticed a road that backed up to the Sampson ranch. It ran along the back of the property. I wondered if I'd be able to go around that way and then sneak onto the ranch. The sun was now setting. It was certain I'd be traveling back to town after dark. It wasn't something I was looking forward to. And if I was smart, I would head back to Abilene right now. But I was stubborn. I represented the law, and I had a job to do. I'm sure the sheriff wouldn't have minded if I had returned without talking to the Sampson kids. But *I* wasn't okay with it. If I waited until dark, it would be easier to make it without being seen. The problem was that the little boy, Theodore, would probably be in the house at that time, and not in the barn. I needed to be able to talk to him from his current location. And that meant I'd better move quickly.

I turned Shuffle and headed back to the ranch, but using the back road this time. I could still see horses and livestock along the new route, but I was a couple of hundred yards away from them. I continued to circle around the property until I was directly behind the barn. I was still probably a good quarter of a mile away from it. But I was afraid of getting any closer on horseback. I pulled on the reins to stop Shuffle. I hopped down and tied her to a small tree. I would have a better chance of sneaking in on foot. Since the grass was high, it provided great camouflage. I jogged for a while until I was no more than about fifty yards away. Then I climbed over a fence and tiptoed my way to the barn. I needed to get to the opposite side to get in. I dropped to my stomach and slithered around the side of the barn until I could see the double doors. I looked over at the farmhouse as well as the surrounding area. I didn't see anyone. It was time to make my move. I took one last glance, sprinted to the open door, and snuck inside.

It was dark. My eyes needed a few seconds to adjust. When they did, I was staring directly at young Theodore. He was standing there with a pitchfork in his hands.

"Don't come any closer or I'll use this thing," he said.

I held up my hands. "I'm not going to hurt you. I just want to talk to you."

"My father told you to get off our property. He said I'm not allowed to talk to you."

"But it's really important," I said. "Are you a friend of Tommy Walker?"

"Why?"

"Because he's in trouble, and he needs your help."

"I don't believe you," the boy said.

"It's true, Theodore."

"That's not my name," he snapped. "My name is Teddy."

"Teddy, yesterday afternoon, Tommy and Abigail Walker were working in their fields when something awful happened to them." I needed to gain his trust. I figured if I kept talking about his friend, and about the trouble he was in, then Teddy might eventually warm up to me.

"What happened to them?" he asked.

"We're not sure. And that's why we need your help."

"Well, I don't know anything about them," he said. "How can I help?"

"Can you remember the last time you saw Tommy?"

Teddy thought to himself for a moment. "I might have seen him yesterday."

"You might have?"

"It's hard to remember. We were riding in my dad's buckboard when I think we saw them."

"Them?"

"Tommy *and* Abby."

I heard a voice coming from the farmyard, and it appeared to be getting closer. I wasn't sure what to do. It was higher-pitched. It had to be a female voice. I moved up against the wall of the barn near the door. I needed to position myself for a quick exit.

"Teddy, it's time for dinner," the voice said. It was a girl about eleven or twelve years old. She was standing in the doorway. It must be his sister, Susan, I thought. I remained perfectly still. "Well, c'mon, let's go," she said.

"What about *him*?" Teddy said, pointing at me.

Oh, no. I had been outed.

CHAPTER 13

Susan backpedaled a few feet. "Who are you? And what are you doing in here?"

"My name is Pete Moss, and I'm working with Sheriff Malone. We're investigating the disappearance of two of your neighbors." This was when I really wished I had a badge.

"Who's missing?" she said.

"Abby and Tommy Walker. They haven't been seen since yesterday afternoon."

"Don't you remember, Sue," Teddy said. "I think we saw them yesterday when we were out with father."

"Yeah, there was a boy with them, I think. He was leading them somewhere."

This was great stuff. I needed to keep pressing.

"A boy? Did you recognize him?"

"No, his back was to me most of the time," Susan said.

"Could you tell how old he was?"

"About my age, I guess."

I thought to myself for a moment. What kind of kid was capable of something like this? And then I remembered what I had heard about Fred Kimball. Had he taken them? Was he hiding them somewhere?

"Do you suppose the boy could have been...Fred Kimball?"

"How do you know about him?" Susan asked.

"Some of your classmates have mentioned him," I said. "And they haven't had very nice things to say."

"There's nothing nice about Fred."

"Do you think it could have been him then?"

Susan paused. "Well, the boy was about the same height and weight as Fred, but I couldn't be a hundred percent sure."

That was good enough for me. I knew, for better or worse, my next stop would have to be the Kimball house. Fred sounded like a prime suspect. I wasn't sure I wanted to tangle with him alone though. I decided to head back to Abilene tonight and see if the sheriff would accompany me to Fred's house tomorrow.

"Do you think they're all right?" Teddy said.

"I sure hope so. You guys have been a huge help. One more question—do you remember which direction this boy was leading Abby and Tommy?"

Teddy pointed to his left.

"Yeah, that sounds right," Susan said.

I wasn't exactly sure which direction that was. "To be honest, I'm still trying to get my bearings around here. What direction would that be?"

"Due east," Susan said.

"And one more thing. Can you point me toward Abilene. I'm headed there tonight."

"You're riding back to town...tonight...by yourself...in the dark?" Susan said.

"Yeah, it's better than making camp somewhere in the middle of the prairie," I said.

"You can't go by yourself tonight. I'll ask my dad if you can stay with us."

I held my hands up. "No, don't do that! He made it very clear that I wasn't welcome here. He kicked me off your property a little while ago. I'm not sure what he might do if he knew I had snuck back and talked to you guys."

"Well, you can't go out there alone at night," Susan said.

"Maybe he could stay in here," Teddy said.

"No, that's okay," I said. "It's very nice of you, but—"

"It's all settled. You can sleep over there. In stall number four."

I wasn't sure what to do. Should I try to make it back to town by myself in the dark? Or should I risk getting caught by Mr. Sampson who might do who knows what to me if he finds me in here? Neither sounded particularly appetizing.

"How did you get here?" Susan said. "I didn't see a horse anywhere. You didn't walk, did you?"

"I rode," I said. "I left my horse about a quarter mile back there." I pointed toward the back of the barn.

"Teddy, you go tell dad there's something I have to do. Tell him I'll be in for dinner in a few minutes." She turned to me. "C'mon."

"Where are we going?" I asked.

"You'll never find your horse by yourself. I'll go with you."

"And you won't tell your dad I'm sleeping here tonight?"

"No, of course not." She turned to Teddy. "Not a word to Father about this," she said. "You understand?"

He nodded.

Susan reflected for a moment. "On second thought, I think you oughta sleep up in the loft. Less chance of anyone finding you."

"Whatever you say."

Teddy ran out of the barn. Susan and I headed out to where I had left Shuffle. It was now pitch black outside, and on top of that, it had gotten foggy. I had no idea how I would have found my way back to town in this soup.

"There are few rabbit holes out here," she said. "Be careful not to step in them or you'll for sure sprain an ankle."

I walked directly behind her, step by step. She seemed to know exactly where she was going. I followed carefully. At one point, there was a lull in the conversation. I decided to take a chance and ask her a personal question.

"Susan, you talk about your dad a lot. Is your mom around?"

She turned around and stopped. "My mother is dead. She died giving birth to Teddy." She continued on without a peep.

"I'm sorry I asked. It was none of my business."

"It's all right," she said. "For a while there, I was mad at Teddy. I blamed him for Mother's death. But one thing I've learned—childbirth is dangerous. The same thing happened to a few of my kin. I'm not sure I'll ever have children."

Having a baby was something I had taken for granted. Back home, with the help of modern medicine, very few women died giving birth. I forgot there were no guarantees when you were having a baby in the Old West.

Susan pointed to where I had tied up Shuffle. "Is that her?"

"Yep."

"She's pretty. Where'd you get her?"

"Well, she actually belonged to Sheriff Malone. So, when the sheriff got a new horse, he gave me his." I untied Shuffle from the tree. "*You* should ride him. I'll walk."

"He seems strong enough to handle both of us."

I hopped on, and then reached my hand down to help Susan up. She grabbed hold and swung herself aboard. She put her hands around my waist to hold on. I liked how it felt. She directed me back to the barn in the dark. When we got there, she took Shuffle's saddle off and tied him up in one of the stalls.

She pointed up to the loft. "Head up there and find a nice soft spot to bed down. I'll try to sneak you out some dinner when I can."

"Thanks a lot. I really appreciate this."

"It's fine. Don't worry." She stopped and stared at me momentarily. "By the way, how does someone your age end up working in the sheriff's office?"

"Oh, well, that's a long story. Remind me to tell you about it sometime." I smiled.

"I'll see you in a little bit."

Susan left the barn and I climbed up a rickety ladder to the loft. It smelled only slightly better up there. I found a spot in the corner and began bunching up some loose hay to create a makeshift bed. I then built a wall around me with bales of hay to stay better hidden. I lay down on my side to rest but got jabbed again by that same darn magnet in my pocket. I had half a mind to throw it away. I couldn't imagine an instance where I'd need a magnet in the Old West. I slid it out of my pocket and stared at it.

And then just as I was about to heave it into a pile of hay, I stopped. What if I did need this thing for some reason? If I got rid of it, it wouldn't be there in a jam. What was wrong with me? Why was it so hard to make a decision? I put the magnet back into my pocket. Before long I had managed to doze off. I might have slept there for hours had not a voice awakened me sometime later.

"Pete? Pete, are you up there?" It was Susan.

I woke with a start and crawled over to where the ladder was. "Hi."

"I have some supper for you. Can I bring it up?"

"Sure. Or I can come down to get it."

"No, you'd better stay up there. I don't want my father finding you." She held the plate of food with one hand while climbing the ladder with the other. When she got near the top, I reached down and grabbed the plate and then pulled her up. She noticed the little hiding place I had built. "That was pretty smart," she said. We sat down on some hay, and I removed a cloth napkin that was covering the food.

I leaned in to take a whiff. "Smells great," I said. "What is it?"

"Roasted potatoes and muskrat."

"Muskrat?" My voice squeaked. "I haven't had the pleasure."

"You've never eaten muskrat? Where are you from anyway?"

"Um, Wichita."

"You're from Wichita and you've never eaten muskrat?"

I wasn't sure how to answer that. "We're mostly rabbit people," I said. I looked down at the plate in my lap and dug in. I ate all of the potatoes first. Then I forced myself to try the muskrat. I picked up a piece and bit into it. It wasn't bad, although it didn't taste like anything I had ever eaten before. "It's good," I said. "Did you make it?"

"I do all the cooking," she said. "After all, I am the lady of the house."

"So, how old are you?" I tried to swallow before speaking.

"I'll be twelve next week."

"I'm twelve. So, what grade at school are you in?" I asked.

"I just finished sixth."

"Me too. Is your school around here."

"Uh-huh. It's a one-room schoolhouse about two miles up the road."

"Did you say *one-room*?"

"Well, yeah. Isn't your school in Wichita the same?"

I had to think fast. I couldn't imagine being in the same room with younger kids and older ones. I saw a lot of problems with that setup. When your teacher was working with *your* grade level, how would the other kids in the room manage to concentrate. It had to be so distracting.

"Now that you mention it...it is one room. I'm not sure why I asked. So, where do you plan on going to high school?"

"High school?"

"You know, ninth through twelfth grade?"

"Oh, I'll be done with school after eighth grade."

"But if you don't go to high school, how will you get into college."

She laughed. "College? Don't be silly. I'm a girl. Girls don't go to college."

Girls don't go to college? I couldn't believe what I was

hearing. It just didn't make any sense. How were they supposed to support themselves when they got older?

"How will you pay your bills when you grow up without a college education?" I said.

She cocked her head to one side and had a puzzled look on her face. "Well, I'll marry someone who has a job. That's how."

Wow, this sure wasn't the time to be a girl. I wanted to tell her how far women had advanced back where I came from, but I knew it would be too hard for her to understand. Heck, being here in the Old West was hard enough for me to understand.

The sound of the barn door sliding open froze both of us.

"Shhh, duck down," she whispered.

I fell onto my stomach and held my breath.

"Susan? Where are you?" her father said.

"Up here." She waved to her dad.

"What are you doing up there?"

She paused momentarily. "Just thinking. I come up here to think sometimes."

"Well, you can do all your thinking in the kitchen while you're washing the dishes. Now get down here."

She waved to me before climbing down the ladder. A moment later, Susan and her dad were gone. The barn door had been closed and locked from the outside. It looked like I'd be spending the next few hours up here whether I liked it or not. I glanced at the plate of unfinished muskrat and made a face. I was definitely done with that. I rolled over, fell onto my back, and put my hands behind my head. I thought about everything that had happened since I had magically arrived in Abilene, Kansas in 1888. I couldn't believe I was working alongside my hero, Sheriff Amos *Lone Wolf* Malone. I didn't think I'd ever be able to tell anyone about this experience. Certainly not my parents. They would think I needed to talk to a shrink. I probably couldn't even tell Will. Even though he was my best friend, he would never believe me if I told him how I exited through a secret passageway in the basement of the library and ended up back in the Old West.

The more my mind wandered, the more I found myself thinking about how the sheriff's life would be snuffed out at a poker game on July 11th. Even though he would fight me, and would probably refuse to listen, I knew I had to tell him about what would happen that night. I just couldn't let a man as decent as Sheriff Malone die before his time. I closed my eyes and eventually drifted off. I would manage to stay fast asleep until I was rudely awakened in what seemed like the middle of the night.

I jumped when I heard the barn door slide open. I could hear voices below. I lay perfectly still. It sounded like more than one person. I snuck a peek and saw Mr. Samuelson holding a silver metal bucket. Susan was by his side. He handed her the bucket and pointed to a cow in the middle stall.

"Time to get to work," he said.

I soon figured out she was here to milk their cow. This girl really worked hard, I thought. I didn't think I certainly didn't think I was cut out to work on a farm in these times. I was sure glad my place was in the sheriff's office. I watched as Mr. Sampson headed to the open barn door. About halfway there, he stopped and stared.

"Susan! Where did that horse come from?"

Uh oh. He was talking about Shuffle. If he somehow

remembered I was riding that horse yesterday, my days on this earth would be numbered. I was hoping Susan could talk her way out of this.

"Oh," she said. "That's one of...Annie's horses."

"Annie who?"

"I go to school with her."

"So, why is one of her horses in our barn?"

Susan cleared her throat. She was thinking on the fly. "They had some family members visiting and they ran out of space in their barn. I told her it would be okay for Thor to stay here tonight. She'll be stopping by this morning to pick him up."

"And you didn't think to tell me about it?"

"Well...I assumed you'd be okay with it."

He sighed and shook his head. "Next time, ask first."

"Yes, Father."

Mr. Sampson turned and left the barn. Susan ran over to the ladder.

"Pete? Are you awake?"

I peeked out. "You are one great fibber. I don't think I could have come up with a story like that so quickly."

"When you lie, you break one of the commandments." She seemed embarrassed. "I'm not proud of myself. But it was just easier this way. And a lot better for you."

"You're tellin' me. Well, I really appreciate it."

"We'd better get you out of here right now. Come on down."

I started down the ladder.

"I'm sorry I won't have time to make you any breakfast."

"Don't be. It's fine."

She ran over to Shuffle and threw my saddle onto her

back. She reached under his belly and tightened the straps. She ran to the barn door and looked out.

"It looks like Father's in the house. Hurry."

I ran over to Shuffle and jumped on. I turned him toward the door and headed out. I peeked into the farmyard. It appeared empty.

"You know where you're going, right?" she said.

"I think so."

"Just go back the same way you came last night."

"Okay," I said. "Thanks for everything. I hope I see you again sometime."

"Me too." She smiled. "I hope you find Abby and Tommy."

"Don't worry. We will." I tipped my hat and grinned. It had been so worth it to come here. I grabbed the reins and took off. Next stop—Abilene.

CHAPTER 14

ONCE I WAS SURE I WAS OFF THE SAMPSON PROPERTY AND on the back road, I stopped and pulled out the map. It was still pretty dark out. I could see the sun trying to break through over the eastern horizon. I figured it had to be near five thirty or thereabouts. Normally, if I had gotten up that early, I'd be pretty tired right now, but due to the fact that I probably fell asleep in that hay loft about seven or seven thirty last night, I was well rested. I'd hit the main road in a few minutes, and then took that all the way into Abilene. But since Shuffle needed something to drink, I'd have to make a detour and head for a stream about four or five miles out of the way.

I was thinking what I'd tell the sheriff about my interrogations. I'd start with Fred Kimball. Susan and Teddy Sampson were sure they had seen a boy matching his description leading Abby and Tommy Walker east along the main road. That was the same direction I'd be traveling back to Abilene. I would ask the sheriff to join me for a visit to speak to Mr. Kimball. I only hoped he would agree. Considering his history with that kid, I would think he would be on board. But I wasn't sure if the injured Cheyenne boy would change our plans. By this time, he would be receiving medical attention from Doc Conrad. I sure hoped he pulled through. The big question was—would the sheriff consider finding the missing children more important than tracking down those buffalo hunters? To me, it was a no-brainer. Every minute that passed could spell doom for these kids. But those other two rats? All we had to do was locate the nearest buffalo herd and they'd fall into our laps.

I was now close to the stream. I could hear it bubbling in the distance. I was sure Shuffle would be glad to lap up some tasty spring water. When we got close, I jumped down and walked her up to the water. She immediately began to drink. I felt bad our water breaks were so far apart. I reached for my canteen, took a swig, and then refilled it in the stream. The water was nice and cool. It was hard to believe you could drink water right from a stream or lake. I'd never try that back home. But this was a perfect pick-me-up for a late June day on the hot Kansas prairie. When Shuffle had had her fill, I climbed aboard and we headed back to the main road. When we got there, we hadn't gone more than a mile when I saw a buckboard about a hundred yards in front of us headed in the same direction. When I got close enough to see who was at the reins, I was less than thrilled. It was Mrs. Hailey.

"Well, if it ain't the new boy who's been helpin' out the sheriff," she said. "Headed into town for more licorice root? I sure am."

I suddenly remembered our conversation at the General Store a few days earlier. "But I thought you said you didn't like licorice root."

"Oh, it ain't for me," she said. "It's for some friends stayin' with me."

This conversation had already gone on a lot longer than I wanted it to. I wasn't Mrs. Hailey's biggest fan. It was time for a hasty retreat.

"Well, I gotta be heading into town," I said. "Gotta meet up with the sheriff."

"Big meetin', is it?"

"Yeah, we're working on the Walker case."

"What's that all about?" she asked.

"Oh, haven't you heard? Abby and Tommy Walker went missing the other day. No one can find them."

She covered her heart with her hand. "Those sweet youngins. How awful? Well, I'll keep a look out for them. You can be sure o' that. And I'll let the sheriff know if I see anything suspicious."

"Thanks a lot. That would be great. Well, I'll see ya in town." I nudged Shuffle and we were off. We had no problem pulling away from the buckboard. A horse with a lone rider is a lot faster than one pulling a wagon. Right about then, I was beginning to get hungry. I reached into my saddlebag and found one last stale crusty muffin. As brutal as these things were, I had to say it was pretty tasty on an empty stomach. I washed it down with a belt from my canteen. The water was still cool. That would have to hold me until I was able to make it into town. I couldn't wait to sit down to a scrumptious meal at Halsey's. I could only hope that muskrat wasn't on the menu.

I finally made it back to Abilene an hour or so later. It was still relatively early when I rode down Main Street on my way to the sheriff's office. I decided to drop off Shuffle with Jeremiah at the livery stable. She needed a good rubdown, food, water, and rest. And she had earned it. Shuffle had performed like a champ in the field.

On my way to the sheriff's office, I noticed a crowd of people outside Doc Cramer's office. I wasn't sure what was going on. When I saw the sheriff's horse tied to the hitching post outside, I assumed he was at Doc's. I decided to drop in, but I had to squeeze through the crowd of onlookers. I couldn't help but notice that these folks didn't look very happy. A few of them had their guns drawn. What the heck was going on? When I managed to work my way through the mob and was just about to enter Doc's office, I heard a voice directed toward me.

"Hey, boy, I wouldn't go in there if I was you. You might get scalped."

I turned away and was just about to enter the office when I realized the door was locked. That was odd. I decided to knock. I could see someone pull back the curtains on a window inside and look out. It was the sheriff. He immediately unlocked the door, opened it quickly, grabbed me by the shirt, pulled me in, and locked the door.

"What's goin' on out there?" I said.

"The local residents of Abilene don't much take to mendin' a banged-up Indian," the sheriff said.

"Well, what were you supposed to do?" I said. "Leave him there to die?"

"Seems like those folks would have been just fine with that," Doc Cramer said.

"I can't believe it," I said.

"If I refused to patch up every person I didn't like," Doc said, "half of that group out there would be dead."

"These people have no humanity," Sheriff Malone said. "And you can't convince them that an Indian is a person just like them. To these folks, they're savages. And the fewer of them around, the better."

I always knew white settlers and townsfolk back in the 1800s disliked Native Americans, but I never realized how much. Those folks had no problem with running them off their land and claiming it as their own. It was an awful thing to do. The Native American tribes were here first. They had no choice but to defend themselves. It would have been nice if there had been someone to settle these issues. The government didn't protect them. They actually went as far as forcing these first Americans to leave the lands they had settled and live on reservations. It was clearly a form of racism. And it would take decades and decades for it to be resolved—as if it ever was. If you were to ask any Native American today if their people had ever been compensated for the lands taken away from them, they would answer with an emphatic *No*.

"Where's the patient?" I asked. "Is he okay?"

"He's resting in the next room," Doc said. "It looks like he should pull through. But he's in no condition to be moved. Not for a few days."

"Sheriff, what do you plan to do with him?" I asked.

"Once he's healthy enough to travel, I'll take him back to the reservation." He peeked out the window. "If we can ever get out of here alive."

I pointed to the crowd. "How long have they been here?"

"Ever since one of them walked into the office yesterday and spotted the boy," the sheriff said.

"Amos," Doc said, "you're gonna have to stick around here as long as this boy is in the next room. If that crowd outside sees you leave, they'll turn into a lynch mob."

"I don't plan on going anywhere, Doc."

I had wanted the sheriff to join me on a trip to see Fred Kimball. I wasn't sure we could wait for the Cheyenne boy to heal before heading out there.

"By the way, Pete, did you learn anything about the missing children?" the sheriff asked.

"Not a whole lot," I said.

"Hiram Walker stopped in here yesterday and asked if we had found out anything. The man was a wreck. I'm not sure he's slept since those children went missing.

"I did learn something that might be helpful," I said. "A boy who looked a lot like Fred Kimball was seen leading Abby and Tommy down the road right about the time they went missing."

"Where'd you learn this?" the sheriff asked.

"From one of Abby's school friends, Susan Sampson. She and her little brother saw it happen."

"Sampson. I should have warned you about their dad. He has no respect for the law."

"I found that out," I said. "He kicked me off their ranch, but I snuck back last night and talked to the kids."

The sheriff smiled.

"He's turning into a real lawman, Amos," Doc Conrad said.

"He certainly is," the sheriff replied. "Well done, young man."

"Now I have to pay a visit to Mr. Kimball. I was hoping you'd be able to go there with me, but I can see your hands are full."

The sheriff shook his head. "Pete, I'd love to join you, but that's an ugly crowd out there. I can't leave Doc here alone."

"Don't worry. I can handle it."

The sheriff put this hand on my shoulder. "I know you can."

I smiled.

"Now, Pete, I want you to be careful with this Fred Kimball character. He's ornery. He won't much take kindly to being accused of kidnapping those kids. If you think he had something to do with the kidnapping, don't try to bring him in alone. We'll have to wait till this crisis here is over, and then I'll go with you."

"Okay, that sounds good."

"Amos, you picked the perfect time for an apprentice," Doc said. "This way you can handle two emergencies at the same time."

"I'm not sure what I woulda done without Pete here," the sheriff said.

And suddenly I had a brainstorm. This was the perfect time to ask the sheriff for a badge. If I was so indispensable, then how could he say no.

"Sheriff, I have a question for you. Every time I introduce myself to folks and tell them I'm working for you and that I need to ask them some questions, they look at me kind of funny. It's as if they don't believe I'm legit. I was just wondering. Is there any way I could maybe get a badge or something? I'd just use it to prove I work for the sheriff's office. That's all."

Doc Conrad turned to the sheriff and nodded. "He's got a point, Amos."

"He does. You know, for years I'd argue with the US Marshall in Dodge City about whether or not I needed a deputy. He wanted me to have one, but I'd always tell him I was more than capable of handling Abilene's problems myself." He looked at me. "If you're wondering, that's where the *Lone Wolf* nickname came from."

"You're kidding," I said. "You got it 'cause you preferred working alone?"

He nodded.

"But I've been giving that a lot of thought lately. Since you've worked out so well, I'm reconsidering my need for a deputy."

"I know the perfect candidate," Doc said.

"Me too." He grinned. "Pete, I want you to go over to the office, sit down at my desk, and open the third drawer on the right. You'll find a Bible. Underneath it in a brown envelope is a badge—a deputy badge. I want you to wear it."

"Really?! Are you serious?"

"I am. You've earned it."

"Can I go get it now?" I said.

"Sure," the sheriff said. "But you'd better go out the back way. I don't want you to have to deal with that hostile mob outside."

I ran to the back door and stopped. I needed a way to thank him for the badge. I knew just the way.

"How about if I stop by the diner on my way back and pick up some lunch for the two of you?"

Doc grinned. "Now that's a marvelous idea." He turned to the sheriff. "What's the special today?"

The sheriff put his finger to his lips. "Let's see. Today's Wednesday. So, it should be pot roast. Doc, what do you say?"

"Thank God it's not Thursday," Doc said. He made a face. "Rabbit Stew."

"Pete, on your way back, rustle up a couple of those pot roast dinners for us, and get whatever you want. Tell Darla to put it on the sheriff's tab."

"Will do." Before I was out the door, a rock came flying

through the front window, shattering it into a million pieces. A couple of flying shards nicked the sheriff on the side of the head.

"This is getting out of control," the sheriff said. He pointed at me. "Pete, go. Hurry up."

I ran out the back door and eventually worked my way onto Main Street. I walked around the building and was soon out in front. The crowd had unfortunately grown. I could hear murmurs from people wanting to rush the sheriff, take the Cheyenne boy, and string him up. Things were definitely getting out of control. I stood there for a minute and tried to blend in. I was hoping to get some information I could share with the sheriff. When I looked up, I saw the door opening and the sheriff step out onto the street. He was holding a rifle.

"I don't suppose you're gonna tell me who threw that rock, now are you?" Sheriff Malone said.

First there was silence. Then an overweight man who hadn't shaved in quite a while stepped forward.

"His squaw mother thrown it," he said. "She wants him to know it's time for lunch." He and his fellow troublemakers broke into laughter.

"Very funny, fellas," the sheriff said. "Now why don't you all just head home. The show's over. I'm sure you have better things to do with your time than loiter on a public street."

"We ain't goin' nowhere until that Injun comes out," another voice said.

"The boy's in bad shape," the sheriff said. "He's not goin' nowhere."

"We got a little reception planned for him," someone called out. "And it don't matter what shape he's in."

The sheriff cocked his rifle. "Once he's healed up, I'm

going to return him to the reservation. So, you can all just break things up and get on outa here."

"That ain't happenin', Sheriff. And if you know what's good for you, you'd better just step aside and hand him over."

"If you want that boy, you're gonna have to go through me," the sheriff said. "And you all know me. I won't back down. You might succeed in getting past me, but I guarantee I'll take down at least a half dozen of you."

It suddenly got very quiet. Things were at a stalemate. Everyone was frozen in place. Then a man finely dressed in a suit and a derby stepped up.

"All right, sheriff, we'll send some of our party home, but we're gonna leave a contingent right here in case you try to sneak that savage out." He turned to the man standing next to him. "Jerry, you and some of the boys stay right here. We'll spell you in a few hours." He looked at the sheriff. "You gotta sleep sometime, Amos. But me and the boys can take shifts. We can wait you out. You'll see."

Some members of the crowd began to disperse, but a handful remained in place. This wasn't over by a longshot. I decided to sprint over to Halsey's and get a jump on the lunch crowd. When I arrived, a few folks were standing in the doorway looking down the street at the commotion in front of Doc's office. I slipped in, found a waiter, and asked for Darla. A woman in a white dress with a lot of ruffles walked over.

"What can I do for you, honey?"

"Can I get three orders of pot roast to go. And can you charge it to the sheriff?"

"I think I can do that," she said. "It'll be about ten minutes. Do you have something else in town you can do while we make up those plates?"

I was just about to tell her that I'd wait there when I remembered the badge. "Sure, I'll be back in ten minutes."

"Okay, just come up to the counter and ask for me when you get back."

"Thanks." I left the restaurant and headed down the street to the sheriff's office. When I got there, I made a beeline for the desk. I opened the third drawer on the right and spotted the Bible. I lifted it up, and just like the sheriff had said, I found an envelope underneath. I opened it and poured out the contents on the desktop. There were two badges. One was a sheriff's badge. Wouldn't be needing that. The other one was all brass. It was in the shape of a six-pointed star. On it were the words: *Deputy Sheriff – Abilene, Kansas*. I put the sheriff's badge back in the envelope and placed it in the drawer with the Bible. I took the deputy badge and pinned it to my shirt. I walked over to a mirror and admired it. I had to say it looked great. Now maybe I'd get a little respect whenever I asked to speak to someone.

I ran back to Halsey's and picked up the grub. As I was walking back to Doc's office, I thought about the Cheyenne boy. I hadn't picked up any food for him. I wondered if I should go back and ask for more pot roast. Then I wondered if he was healthy enough to eat. Maybe that was why Doc hadn't asked me to get anything for him. When I got close to the office, most of the people who had been standing outside were gone. Only about five or six men were milling around by the front door. Rather than mixing in with them, I went around back. I knocked twice and the sheriff answered.

He took a whiff. "Smells great." He held the door open for me.

I walked into the waiting room and set the plates

down on a table. For the next twenty minutes or so, Doc, Sheriff Malone and I wolfed down the somewhat tough pot roast. I just listened to their conversation. It was mostly about the crowd outside and various ways they'd be able to sneak the Cheyenne boy out and back to the reservation. Since the patient was in no shape to travel, there didn't seem to be any sense of urgency. The sheriff was hoping the men standing outside would eventually get tired and head home at some point. But he knew that wouldn't happen right away. They were pretty angry and probably wouldn't back down for some time.

"I suppose we oughta discuss the Walker situation," the sheriff said. "Pete, how many of those families have you talked to?"

"Three."

"How many do you have left?"

"Three more. Not including Fred Kimball." I knew I should really be making Fred Kimball more of a priority, but I wasn't sure I wanted to face him alone. I wasn't overly big for my age, and I was no authority in the art of fisticuffs. I wasn't sure how he'd react when I told him he had been seen leading the missing persons off their farm. I didn't think he'd be too happy to hear that. Since I still had three more of Abby's friends to speak to, I thought I might be able to milk those interviews for a few days. Maybe then the sheriff would have returned the Cheyenne boy to his reservation, and he'd be available to accompany me to the Kimball house. That sounded like a plan.

"Pete, maybe you should skip those last three families, and go directly after Fred Kimball."

Oh, no. That would screw up all my plans. I needed to

persuade him to stay the course and not rush into anything.

"But what if one of the kids we haven't spoken to yet can give us some critical information to solve this case."

"To be honest, I don't think that's gonna happen. I'm worried that while you're talking to these other families, the real kidnapper may be getting further away or doing something awful to those children. The possible Fred Kimball sighting is the best piece of information we've been able to gather so far. I think we have to move on that. Okay?"

I nodded. But I was dreading it. I didn't know why I was acting like such a wuss. I had spent most of my life reading about tough, macho, fearless lawmen who had tamed the Old West. I had always imagined myself as one of them or fighting alongside them. But now when I found myself facing a critical moment in my life, why did I feel so inadequate? I had to step up my game. I had to stop feeling sorry for myself and start thinking about Abby and Tommy. Every minute they spent away from home in unspeakable conditions has to have been awful for them. And here I was whining about facing a bully. They were so much braver than I was. I needed to show them I could meet this challenge. I needed to demonstrate that a kid who lived a hundred and thirty-plus years in the future had the same courage as the lawmen in the 1880s. Now was the time to show my stuff. I only hoped I had the wisdom to solve this case, and the backbone to face my enemies and save those kids.

CHAPTER 15

AFTER LUNCH I SPENT THE REMAINDER OF THE DAY WALKING around observing the townsfolk. Sheriff Malone had asked me to be his eyes and ears while he was at Doc's. I prayed there would be nothing that might require the sheriff's attention. If so, he'd have to leave Doc and the Cheyenne boy unprotected. If that occurred, the lynch mob outside would surely make their move. I decided to poke my head into the General Store and who did I meet there but Mrs. Hailey. She was buying some licorice root for her house guests.

"Well, fancy seeing you again," she said.

"Hi, how are you?"

"You any closer to finding those missing children?" she asked.

"No, not yet. But we're still looking."

She looked around to make sure no one could hear what she was about to say. She leaned in and whispered.

"If I were you, I'd head out to that reservation and tear the place apart. I wouldn't put anything past those redskins. And I should know. I've lived through it."

"Well, thanks for the suggestion," I said. "I'll talk to the sheriff about it." But I had no intention of doing so. This woman had a reputation for blaming the Native Americans for things that never happened. I wished she would just butt out and let the law handle this.

I continued on, keeping my eyes open the entire time. I peeked into the saloon without going in. Some of the troublemakers who had been standing outside Doc's office were in there talking trash about the Cheyenne boy. After a while, I had to leave. I couldn't take any more of it. I walked back to the office and thought about what was facing me tomorrow. The plan was to head to Fred Kimball's place in the morning. I was to question him in a *non-threatening way* as the sheriff put it. He wanted me to try to trip him up, but not to accuse him of anything that might set him off. I wasn't exactly sure how to go about doing that. As I sat in the sheriff's office that night, I rehearsed the types of questions I would ask. I imagined myself grilling him and eventually breaking him. He would then offer to take me to a shack where he had been hiding the kids. Then when I got there, I'd find Abby and Tommy bound and gagged. I would immediately untie them and Abby would throw her arms around me. Everything was working out great—in my head, that was.

I was rather restless that night. I couldn't seem to get comfortable. Since the sheriff wasn't around, I decided to put my mattress on top of his and sleep that way with more cushion under me. It worked pretty well. I eventually drifted off and woke up the next morning about seven a.m. I got cleaned up and headed over to the restaurant. I ordered three breakfast specials—eggs, roasted potatoes, and a slab of bacon. Doc and the sheriff were thrilled to see the feast I had delivered. While there, I learned the

Cheyenne boy was now conscious, and had regained some of his strength. Doc had made broth from some of the leftover pot roast and fed it to him.

"Have you got the map with you?" the sheriff asked.

I pulled it out of my pocket and handed it to him.

He pointed to Abilene. "Here's where we are now." Then he moved his finger to a spot eight to ten miles due south. "And here's where you're headed. Do you think you can find it?"

"It looks easy enough," I said.

"Now remember what I told you. Take it slow and easy with this kid. He's a hothead. And he won't like being questioned."

"I'll be careful," I said.

"After that, you might want to head here." He pointed to an X near a spot called Roberts Gulch. Under it was written *Mabel Greene*. She's another one of Abby's friends. But after talking to Fred, if you think there's enough evidence to arrest him, hurry back here. I don't want you to try to bring him in alone. You might get hurt."

I wished the sheriff wouldn't talk like that so much. He was making me nervous. I had dealt with bullies at school in the past. The best advice on how to handle them came from my buddy, Will. He told me never to let them think they're getting to you. Once they know that, they'll continue to tease you relentlessly. Don't give them the satisfaction of thinking they've ruffled your feathers. Just smile and let it roll off your back. You do that enough times and they'll eventually get frustrated when they're not getting the reaction they hoped for. Pretty soon, they'll just move on to their next victim.

I had used his advice to perfection with a kid named Hank Bradford in fifth grade. That jerk for some reason had it in for me. He used to make fun of my obsession with the Old West. One day I finally got up enough nerve to confront him. "You know, Hank," I said, "you're right, I'm a freak. I enjoy something that other people think is silly. And that's perfectly fine with me. No matter what anyone else says, I'll never give it up. Not in a million years. So, go ahead. Make fun of me. See if I care. Oh, by the way, have a nice day." Afterward, he just stood there—stunned. Whenever he teased me, I just smiled. Pretty soon, he stopped bothering me. It was no fun for him anymore.

I wondered if I had the guts to stand up to Fred Kimball like that. We'd soon find out. I left Doc's office through the back door and walked over to the livery stable. Jeremiah had Shuffle saddled up and ready to go. She looked refreshed. She'd been brushed down, fed, and watered. And she had had a good night's sleep. I glanced at the map and headed south to the Kimball house. As I was leaving town, I looked back down Main Street to see a handful of men still standing in front of Doc's office. I wondered when they'd just get tired and go home. It looked like the sheriff would have his hands full for some time—which meant I was on my own for the foreseeable future. I doubted if he'd be available anytime soon to help bring in Kimball. Listen to me, I hadn't even talked to the kid, and I was ready to haul him in. That might eventually happen but if I ever wanted to be a respected lawman in this town, I would need to be less judgmental. After all, doesn't the saying go something like *innocent until proven guilty?*

The temperature must have been eighty degrees when I set out. It promised to reach the midnineties by noon. I had packed two canteens just in case I managed to use one up too quickly. I would need to keep my eyes open for a watering hole for Shuffle. Heat was as hard on horses as it was on people, according to Jeremiah. If I wasn't able to find a spot, I knew where a stream ran through the prairie. It was a little out of the way, but it would do in a pinch. The entire time, I hadn't seen a single person on the road. There was one thing I had learned in the past couple of weeks. Kansas was flat—mostly plains and prairie with farms and ranches scattered throughout. But not a lot of people.

I had traveled nine or so miles when I spotted fencing and a ranch house in the distance. If the map was correct, I was about to encounter the one and only Fred Kimball. I had heard a lot about him in the last couple of days—and most of it bad. When I got closer, I could see a couple of cowboys in a corral busting some broncos. I couldn't get over the way those horses bucked and threw their riders. That was one occupation I had no interest in. It seemed like you spent more time on your butt than you did on your horse. I decided I had better head toward the ranch house and get this over with. There appeared to be a couple of men standing in front talking. I would start there and hope for the best. When I got close, I hopped off Shuffle and walked up to them. Before I could even introduce myself, one of them spotted the badge. He tried to grab it, but I pulled away.

"So, what do we have here?" he said. He squinted as he examined my badge. "You want me to believe you're a deputy sheriff from Abilene? I thought old Lone Wolf worked all by his lonesome. He ain't never taken on a deputy before."

"He changed his mind," I said.

"And you work for the sheriff?" the second man said.

"Yes."

"What are you doin' here?" he asked. "We ain't broke no laws."

"I'm here to see Fred Kimball. I have a few questions for him."

"So, yer lookin' for Freddie, huh?" the first man said.

I nodded.

He pointed to the corral. "You see that cowpoke sittin' on his beehind...well, that's Freddie. Do me a favor. Ask him when he's gonna start workin'?"

It appeared old Fred Kimball had a reputation wherever he went.

"Thanks." I grabbed Shuffle's reins and walked over to the corral.

Fred was sitting on the fence facing the broncos.

When I was a couple of feet away, I cleared my throat. He turned around.

"Who are you?" he said.

"My name's Pete...Pete Moss." Before I could utter another word, he lit into me.

"Pete Moss?" He laughed. "Yer kiddin' me, right? Who names their kid *Pete Moss*?"

I decided to take the high road. "Well, my parents had an unusual sense of humor."

"That has to be the stupidest name I ever heard of."

"Fred, I'm a deputy sheriff from Abilene, and I—"

"You ain't no sheriff!"

"I didn't say I was the sheriff. I said I was the *deputy* sheriff. There's a difference."

"I know that. I ain't stupid."

I shook my head. This was going to be a nightmare. "I need to ask you a few questions about some missing children."

"Go ahead. Ask. I don't know nothing."

That was obvious. "Are you familiar with Abby and Tommy Walker?"

"Never heard of 'em."

"You never heard of them? That seems strange since you go to school with Abby."

"Oh, that Abby. What about her?"

"She and her brother disappeared a couple of days ago."

"So," he said, "what's that got to do with me?"

"You were seen with them right before they disappeared." I wasn't sure if I should have been so direct but he was making me so mad.

"Who said that? He's a liar."

"I can't tell you who said it."

He grabbed me by the shirt. "I asked you *who said that*?"

Okay. Now this thing had turned physical. This was just what I was hoping to avoid. Fred stood a foot taller than me and at least twenty-five pounds heavier. But I couldn't let him get away with this. He had no right to manhandle a lawman.

I pulled his hand away. "You do that again, and you'll be sorry."

"Oh, really?" he said. "Just what are you gonna do to me?"

"It's considered *assault* to put your hands on a lawman." I had no idea what I was saying, but it sounded good, so I decided to run with it.

"You're a lawman? What are you? Twelve?" He got right in my face.

"Age isn't important," I said. "Now listen, Mr. Kimball, you're a lot bigger than me. And you might be able to kick the crap out of me. But you're not just beating up some kid, you're messing with the law." I fingered my badge. It was time to see if it was going to save my neck. "You see this badge. It just doesn't represent a person. It represents the city of Abilene, and surrounding territory, and the entire state of Kansas. You lay a hand on me, and you have no idea the kind of trouble you'd be in. The sheriff would be after you. The US Marshall would be after you. Heck, the Cavalry would be after you. So, why don't you just be a good boy and answer my questions." I could feel my heart beating right through my chest. I had just rattled off a lot of gobbledygook. I didn't know what I was saying. I just wanted to sound official. I only hoped he would buy it.

Fred took a step backward. "I never saw either of them kids. And whoever told you I was with them is plum lying." He put his hands on his hips and sighed. "I don't know what else to tell you."

Fred sounded like a guilty man, but without some conclusive evidence or a confession, there was no proof he had done anything wrong. I couldn't very well go back and tell the sheriff

we should bring him in and arrest him. Arrest him for *what*? Neither Susan nor Teddy Sampson were sure it was him. My interrogation had failed. I had hoped to trip him up—to get him to say something he would later regret. But he just played dumb—something he was very good at.

"Well, just so you know. You're on our list of suspects. And we'll be back."

"Just so *you* know, if you come back, you'll get the same answers." He stood there with his arms folded smirking.

"You know, you'd feel a lot better if you got this off your chest," I said.

"If you're done with me, I got work to do." He turned and walked away.

I felt like I had completely screwed this up. I had two witnesses who *thought* they had seen him with the missing kids. I should have accomplished more with that information. But I had blown it. I had no more evidence than I had come here with. I jumped back on Shuffle. I didn't even feel like visiting the other families. I was so sure I'd be able to return to the sheriff with enough information to make an arrest and hopefully close this case. I guess I was a rookie, and it showed.

I rode up the long dirt path along the side of the corral to the main road at the top of the hill. I pulled back on the reins and brought Shuffle to a stop. I pulled out the map. There were three different farms I could visit. I wasn't excited about going to any of them. What more could I learn that I hadn't already learned about this case? There wouldn't be any more leads like the Fred Kimball one. That should have been the home run. Instead, here I was licking my wounds. I sat there for a couple more minutes unsure of what to do when I noticed something in the high grass. Whatever it was, I hadn't spotted it on my way in. I hopped off Shuffle and walked with her over to the object. I reached down and picked it up.

Suddenly my heart began to race. This was it. This was the proof I had been looking for. I was staring at a doll— the same doll that Mr. Walker had described. It was Matilda—Abby's doll—the one she carried around all the time. Like her father had said, the doll was about eight inches tall, wearing a red-and-white polka dot dress, with long blond hair. I could see she was dirty. It looked as though she had been through a rainstorm. Her dress was rough and wrinkled. Abby must have dropped it the day she and Tommy were kidnapped. I remember now that it rained that night. Everything was falling into place. Maybe she dropped it on purpose. Abby was a really smart girl. She had to have been leaving us a clue.

I looked over my shoulder. "I'll be back, Fred Kimball. I'll be back with handcuffs." What more proof did we need? Here we were on the corner of the Kimball ranch with the doll that Abby never let out of her sight. She and Tommy had to be on this ranch somewhere. I was sure of it. Now all we had to do was find them.

I jumped back on Shuffle and headed in the direction of Abilene. I rode as quickly as a rookie rider could. I had to share my findings with the sheriff. When he saw the doll, I knew he'd be convinced the kids were on the Kimball ranch. What other conclusion could he draw? But the sheriff had another problem on his hands—trying to protect a frightened, injured Cheyenne boy. How could I convince him to leave Doc's office and join me for a search of the Kimball property? If he did, it might mean certain death for the boy. But if he didn't, it might mean the end of Abby and Tommy. Fred now knew we were hot on his trail. Would he panic and try to get rid of the evidence? I couldn't bear the thought of that. I was sure glad I wasn't the sheriff at this very moment. If I were in his shoes, I wouldn't know what decision to make. Life in 1888 was no easier than it was back in the present. What should I do?

CHAPTER 16

IT TOOK ME THE BETTER PART OF AN HOUR TO GET BACK TO town. When I hit Main Street, I could see there was still a group in front of Doc's office. These guys just wouldn't give up. They were trying to make a point. But all I could see was their hate for Native Americans. This mob complicated things. It meant the sheriff would never leave the Cheyenne boy alone in the office with Doc. They'd both get steamrolled by the crowd. I thought it best to ride around to the alley behind Doc's. When I knocked on the back door, the sheriff answered.

"I didn't expect to see you so quickly," he said.

"Me neither."

"So, how'd you make out with Fred? The fact that you're still in one piece is a good sign."

"My interview with Fred didn't go particularly well. He just denied everything."

"Did he say anything that might have proven his involvement in the abduction?"

"No, not really."

"Did you visit some of Abby's other friends?"

"No. It's not because I didn't want to. It's because I found some evidence linking Fred to the crime."

"What's that?" the sheriff asked.

"When I was just about nearing the end of the Kimball property, I found this in the tall grass." I handed the doll to the sheriff.

He stared at it for a minute. Then a smile seemed to form on his face. "Abby's doll."

"She was there. She and Tommy were right there. Doesn't that prove Fred had something to do with the kidnapping?"

"It might."

"It *might*? Don't you remember Abby's dad telling us she was never without this doll?"

"I do."

"Don't you see? She left it there for us to find."

The sheriff thought to himself for a moment. "You may just be right."

"We have to search the Kimball ranch," I said. "They've got to be there. And we've got to do it as soon as possible. Fred knows we're on to him. He might do anything to keep us from finding the kids."

"Pete, you sound like an alarmist, but in this case you just might be right."

"Okay, now, what do we do? We need a search warrant, right?"

"A what?" the sheriff said.

"A search warrant?"

"What's that?"

And then I realized that law enforcement methods were as advanced back then as they were today.

"Well, it's a piece of paper signed by a judge that lets officers search someone's belongings."

"Why would we need that?" Sheriff Malone said. "We just walk in, show 'em our badges, and search the place."

That sure would make things a whole lot easier. "Okay, when can we go?"

"Not until we take *him* back." The sheriff pointed to the Cheyenne boy who was now standing in the doorway.

"He's better?"

"Thanks to Doc, he is."

Doc came out of the back room and put his hand on the boy's shoulder. "This young man had a strong will to live." He looked at the sheriff. "Amos, he's healthy enough to travel. What's the plan?"

The sheriff pulled back a curtain on the front window. The mob was still in place. "We have to get him back to the reservation as soon as possible. Any day now, that crowd will get impatient and just rush us. That would be the worst possible situation. It would mean bloodshed. And we have to avoid that." He thought to himself for several seconds. "Okay, Pete, this is what I want you to do. I want you to go out the back door and work your way to the sheriff's office. Then I want you to put a change of clothes in a sack and come back here. But this time I want you to use the front door. I want them to know you're in here."

"I have everything but a second pair of boots."

"All right, then. On your way over, stop at the General Store and buy another pair of boots." He glanced at the Cheyenne boy's feet. "Get the same size you have."

"What's going on?" I asked.

"You want to search Fred Kimball's house, right?"

"Yeah, sure."

"Then do this and do it fast."

I didn't ask any more questions. I left through the back

door and streaked to the sheriff's office. When I got there, I looked for a fresh change of clothes. I tossed them in a sack I found on one of the shelves. When I was certain I had everything, I casually walked over to the General Store. I waited for Mr. Crowley to finish up with a customer.

"Excuse me, Mr. Crowley."

"Hi, Pete, how goes the sheriffing business?"

"Oh, just fine. Um...I need a new pair of boots."

He glanced down at the ones I had on. "Those are still in pretty good shape."

"Yeah...well...I'll be doing some pretty strenuous work in the next couple of days, and I'm afraid I'll get these all scuffed up." It was the only thing I could think of.

"I don't want to talk myself out of a sale, but...okay, c'mon over here. So, what are you looking for?"

"Anything is fine," I said. "Just pick whatever."

"Most people are pretty particular about the kinds of boots they wear. You don't care what kind they are?"

"How about another pair of these?" I pointed to my feet.

"Same size?"

"Yeah."

"Hmm, I don't see that size on the shelf. Let me check the back room." He disappeared for a minute, and then returned with a box in his hands. "These are a half size bigger than the ones you're wearing. It's all I've got until a new shipment comes in."

"Those'll be fine."

"You're sure?"

"Yes."

"Okay." He walked over to the cash register. "Is this a charge to the sheriff's office?"

I nodded.

"Do you need a bag or a box?" he asked.

"Neither, I'll just put them in here." I set the sack on the counter and stuffed the boots into it. "Well, thanks a lot. See you later."

"Take care, Pete. Give my best to the sheriff."

I left and headed up the street to Doc's office. When I got there, I could sense I was being watched by the mob out front. I went up to the door and knocked. A moment later, the sheriff appeared in the doorway. When the group saw him, someone in the back yelled out.

"Hey, sheriff, we're not gonna wait much longer."

Sheriff Malone didn't respond. He looked at me and smiled, then closed the door behind us. He peeked into the sack.

"Looks good. Well done."

"Now what?" I asked.

"Now we wait."

"We wait?! But what about Abby and Tommy? Time's running out."

"I haven't forgotten about them," he said. "We're gonna make our move tonight...late."

"So, what's our move?"

"Just sit tight. Relax. Take a nap. Read. Do whatever you like. You gotta be patient. And trust me."

I could tell the sheriff didn't want me asking any more questions. I understood. I knew he had a lot on his mind. The entire time I was sitting there paging through boring magazines, I kept thinking that while we were just sitting around here, something bad may be happening to the Walker kids. I had to trust the sheriff. I put my head back and eventually dozed off. The next thing I knew, Doc was shaking me.

"Wake up, Pete, it's almost dinner time. We need you to go over to Halsey's and pick up four plates of fried chicken."

Did he say *fried chicken*?

"Anything to drink?" I asked.

"We have water and coffee here," Doc said. "And you'll have your hands full with four dinners."

I got up, put on my hat, and headed for the back door.

"No," the sheriff said. "We want them to see you. Go out the front."

I wasn't sure what this was all about, but I switched gears and headed out. I could hear the door lock behind me. A member of the crowd grabbed me by the shirt.

"Hey, kid, what's going on in there?"

"Nothing."

"Don't give me that. Is that filthy savage still in there?"

This guy was so disrespectful. What a jerk. I turned away without answering.

"I'm talking to you, *deputy*," he said.

He had obviously seen my badge. I suppose a good lawman always remained calm and composed—and never let a civilian rile him. I suppose I should have answered that man's question. But until he learned how to respect others, I had no reason to respond. I headed directly for Halsey's. When inside, I looked around for Darla. When our eyes met, she smiled.

"What is it this time, young man?"

"Four fried chicken dinners, please. And you can put them on the sheriff's tab."

She pointed to a chair next to the front door. "If you wanna wait right there, I'll have those dinners out in a few minutes."

I sat down and waited. I kept feeling that some of the

diners were watching me. Maybe they had never seen an official twelve-year-old deputy sheriff before. Some of them may have been scoffing, but that was okay. I sat up straight and smiled. I needed to look confident. I was an important part of two dangerous missions. And nothing these people could say or do would change that. Before I knew it, Darla was hovering over me with four fried chicken plates stacked one on top of the other.

"Here you go," she said. "Enjoy."

"Thank you," I said.

She smiled. "Come back soon."

I left and headed for Doc's office. I squeezed through the crowd which was now about ten men.

"You ain't feedin' that Injun, I hope," someone said.

I just ignored him and walked up to the front door. The sheriff must have seen me coming because the door opened before I was able to knock.

"Hurry, get in here," he said.

When I walked in, I noticed that Doc's desk had been transformed into a dinner table. There was a chair on each of the four sides. At each place there was a napkin, silverware, and a cup of water. In the middle of the table was a lit candle.

"It may not be Halsey's, but it sure ain't bad," the sheriff said.

"It looks kind of formal," I said.

"Well, it's a special night," Doc said. "It's our last meal with Fallen Oak."

"Fallen Oak?" I said.

Doc pointed to the far end of the room. Standing there was the Cheyenne boy.

"That's his name?" I said.

"It is indeed," the sheriff replied. "We had a chance to

talk a little while you were gone. He tells me he's ready to go home." The sheriff said something to the boy in his native tongue. The boy smiled and pulled up a chair. "Well, let's break out those chicken dinners, Pete."

When the sheriff set the meal in front of Fallen Oak, he attacked that bird like he hadn't eaten in months. I doubted if he was accustomed to this type of meal on the reservation. He bit off chunks of chicken and seemed to swallow them whole. He devoured the contents of his plate in what seemed like seconds. Then he guzzled down the cup of water. He wiped his mouth with the back of his hand and let out a long, loud sigh.

"It does my heart good to see this boy's appetite return," Doc said. "When we brought him in here, to tell you the truth, it was touch and go. I wasn't sure he was going to make it. Seeing this is just great."

"You *should* feel great, Doc," the sheriff said. "You're a miracle worker."

"I don't know about that, but I'm sure glad you found this boy when you did. Getting him medical treatment as soon as we did definitely helped save his life."

Once we had all finished our meals, Fallen Oak began to talk, and talk he did. For the next hour or so, we had the most interesting conversation with him. Each word he spoke was translated by Sheriff Malone. It was fascinating, and at the same time, depressing. He talked about the reservation, and how much his people hated it. He longed to live back in a time when the Cheyenne roamed the plains without interference from the white man. The more he spoke, the guiltier I felt. He explained how his tribe had been forced to live on a barren plain without streams or rivers, and with no herds of buffalo. Meat from the buffalo had for decades provided the tribe with much needed food, and the skins were used to make clothing, blankets, and the walls of their teepees. He talked about wandering off the reservation one day in search of wild game when he was spotted by buffalo hunters. He was able to elude them for some time but was ultimately caught and beaten by them. They left him for dead in an old abandoned shack. He told us he would have died had we not found him. He would be forever in our debt.

Afterward, we all sat in Doc's waiting room on the sofa to relax. The sheriff kept looking out the window to check the size of the crowd. He also peeked at his pocket watch frequently. He was waiting for something. We all eventually drifted off and would have remained in that state had not Sheriff Malone awakened us about three a.m.

"Pete, wake up. It's time to go."

"Where?" I said, still half asleep.

The sheriff turned to me. "There's a buckboard and a team of horses all ready to go in the back alley. I want you to go out there and bring it around to the front. There's a tarp in the back of the buckboard. Make it look like there's something hidden under it."

"You want me to bring the rig to the front? Are you sure?" I said.

"I'm positive.

"Are there still people out there?"

"Yeah, but it's okay. Just hurry."

I went out the back door, jumped in the buckboard, and guided it around to the front of Doc's office.

"Goin' somewhere?" someone said as I pulled up.

I just smiled and walked in the front door.

"Okay, Pete, now I want you to go in the next room and change into the clothes you brought with you yesterday."

I followed orders. I grabbed the sack of clothes and

trudged into Doc's examining room. There I changed as quickly as possible. Minutes later when I emerged, I held up the sack, now containing the clothes I had been wearing. "What should I do with these?"

"I'll take that," the sheriff replied. Then he turned to Fallen Oak and spoke to him in Cheyenne. The boy took the sack and walked into the next room.

A few minutes later, Fallen Oak returned. I couldn't believe my eyes. He looked like my exact double. He was dressed in my clothes from head to foot."

The sheriff laughed. He reached over and plucked the hat off my head and put it on the boy's head. He pulled it down so it covered more of his face. Then he stuffed Fallen Oak's long hair under the hat.

"Amos, you're a genius. I never thought you could pull it off. Pete, go over there and stand next to Fallen Oak."

I did as I was ordered.

"It's perfect," Doc said.

"Pete, this is where your Italian heritage pays off," the sheriff said.

"Pete's Italian?" Doc said.

"I'll explain that later," the sheriff replied.

"Wait a minute," I said. "I don't get it."

"Once I saw the resemblance between you two, I knew it could work. Pete, you have dark black hair like Fallen Oak. You also have an olive complexion like Fallen Oak. It's a match made in heaven."

"So, he's going to pretend to be me?" I said.

The sheriff nodded. "Okay, let's do this. Fallen Oak and I are going to go out and get in the buckboard." He turned and said something to the boy. "I told him to keep his head down the entire time. Now, Pete, as soon as you see us pull away, I want you to run out the back door to the edge of town. We'll meet you there. You got it?"

"I think so."

Doc and the sheriff shook hands. "Good luck, Amos."

Sheriff Malone winked. He put his arm around Fallen Oak and opened the front door.

I pulled back the curtain just slightly to watch them. As the two of them walked up to the buckboard in the dark, some members of the mob looked at them suspiciously. One of the men approached.

"So, you're leaving that boy in there unprotected, Sheriff?"

"Yep."

The man noticed the tarp in the back of the buckboard. He ran over, lifted it up, and looked under it.

The man smiled. "Just checkin', Sheriff." He turned to the others. "C'mon, boys. Let's get that Injun."

"I wouldn't do that if I were you," the sheriff said.

"Why not?"

"That Indian boy in there has Scarlet Fever. And I don't have to tell you it's highly contagious. That's why we're getting out."

"What?!"

"Enter at your own risk, gentlemen. So long." The sheriff flicked the reins and the buckboard stormed off.

It was time for me to make my exit. "Well, so long, Doc," I said. "I hope to see you real soon."

"Me, too, Pete. Now get out of here."

I flew out the back door and raced past the rear entrances of several businesses. I kept running until I could see the edge of town. A moment later I spotted the buckboard stopped and waiting for me.

"Let's go," the sheriff yelled.

I jumped up into the back of the buckboard.

The sheriff turned around and smiled. "Now get up into the back and pull that tarp over you. Keep it on until I tell you to come out."

I nodded. I couldn't get over how the sheriff had tricked the townsfolk. Apparently, that was why he was the sheriff and I was only a deputy. Someday I hoped to be able to think as strategically as the sheriff had. I looked over my shoulder in the direction of town. There was no one following us. We had done it. We had actually done it.

CHAPTER 17

WE HAD BEEN RIDING HARD FOR NEARLY AN HOUR AND A half when I noticed just the hint of sun peeking out above the eastern horizon. We were approaching the Cheyenne reservation. You could see the delight in the eyes of Fallen Oak as we got closer. When we crossed a stream of water, he turned to the sheriff and said something. The sheriff nodded. I could only guess he was wishing that stream ran through his reservation. After a few more miles, I saw something I had never seen before. We stopped next to one of them.

"Know where we are, Pete?"

I shook my head.

"This is an official Cheyenne burial ground."

"Are those dead bodies up there?" I asked.

"Yep."

I was staring at a group of what I could only describe as scaffolds that had been built eight or nine feet off the ground. On top of each one was apparently a dead body. Fallen Oak began speaking to the sheriff who translated.

"He says this is how the Cheyenne bury their dead.

They build these structures and place the dead bodies high up close to the sky—close to their gods. He says they often place buckets of food and water on the poles of the scaffolds for the dead. Sometimes toys are left with dead children. And weapons and clothing are placed near the bodies of dead warriors. It would be considered a sacrilege to tamper with any of the bodies." The sheriff turned toward me and smiled. "We're getting a real education from this young man."

I nodded. It *was* pretty cool. And it was even better to see these things first hand. We continued on past the burial grounds and came upon the official entrance to the reservation. A pair of Native Americans holding rifles put their hands up to stop us. The sheriff stood up in the buckboard and spoke to them. They dropped the rifles to their sides. Then Fallen Oak stood and began speaking. They walked up and stared at him. When he removed his, or rather my cowboy hat, they smiled. He jumped down to the ground and they embraced him. This promised to be a great homecoming.

"I asked them to take us to Chief White Deer," the sheriff said. "And then Fallen Oak told them what happened to him out on the prairie, and how we took him into town where Doc brought him back to life."

Cool, I thought.

"You know, Indians aren't particularly fond of the white man's medicine," the sheriff said. "But seeing is believing. They're looking at a happy, healthy young man, and who can argue with that?"

Another Cheyenne tribesman appeared. He apparently would be our escort to see the chief. Fallen Oak hopped back up on the buckboard and we continued on. As we rode through the reservation, I saw a lifestyle I knew very little about. I saw multicolored teepees—what looked like dozens of them. Children ran around with dogs at their heels. Women sat in a circle apparently sewing something—maybe clothes. Men rode up to us on wild ponies. They were riding bareback. They held their right hands up as we passed. I could only assume it meant they viewed us as friends. Other men—braves, I guess—were skinning some sort of large animal, maybe a buffalo or a deer. At one point, the sheriff stopped the buckboard. We were next to one of the larger teepees now.

"Pete, this is it. Come on down and meet Chief White Deer."

I hopped down, as did Fallen Oak. He held open the flap to the entrance of the teepee. We crouched down and entered. Once inside I could see a small fire in the middle. Various animal skins adorned the inside walls. I guessed you called them walls. Seated on the ground next to the fire was an older man. His face was wrinkled. He wore a headdress with hundreds of feathers.

"Sit, my friends," he said.

I couldn't believe he spoke English. This would make it so much easier to know what was going on.

"I've been told of your kindness, Lone Wolf," he said. "Fallen Oak should never have left the reservation alone. There is much danger out there. You will find and punish the men who did this?"

"Chief, you have my word," the sheriff said. "I won't rest until I find those men and put them behind bars."

"That is all I ask. Some of our braves have talked about forming a war party to find these people ourselves. I have told them to wait until I had spoken to you."

"Thank you for that," the sheriff said. "That would

only bring more bloodshed. Trust me, I will find these men and bring them to justice."

"The white man's justice or Cheyenne justice?" the chief said.

"Chief White Deer, justice *is* justice."

The chief smiled. "Is it justice when your courts ignore the truth and set murderers and thieves free?"

"Our court system isn't perfect. I'll grant you that. But it's all we have, and more often than not, the guilty are punished."

"Not always, my friend."

"You're right—not always."

"I will leave this matter in your hands for now. Please let us know when you have caught these men."

"I'll come here personally to let you know," the sheriff said.

"Thank you. Now will you eat with us?"

What exactly did these folks eat, I wondered? Not raw meat or something like that, I hoped.

The chief clapped his hands. A moment later, two women entered carrying plates of food. They set them on the ground in front of us. I couldn't tell what any of it was. I nudged the sheriff.

"Is this stuff safe to eat?" I whispered.

The sheriff chuckled. "Pete, it's all perfectly safe."

"Maybe I'll just pass," I said.

"It would be an insult to our host not to eat with him. Just try some of it. You may be surprised."

I looked across to the chief who had picked up on what was going on. He grabbed for a plate of what looked like meat of some kind. He held it out to me.

"Don't worry, my young friend. Here, try some."

I glanced at the sheriff who nodded at me. I took that

as an order to take some meat. I reached for a piece and smiled politely. Then I brought it to my mouth and bit into it. I chewed and swallowed.

"It's pretty good," I said.

"See," the sheriff said. He turned to the chief. "What kind of meat is this?"

"Beaver," he said.

My jaw dropped. *Beaver?!* Oh, man. What was it about the 1800s that had fascinated me so? Right about now, I wasn't quite sure. I didn't think I could ever get used to some of the foods these people ate. Fortunately, the rest of the meal went down more smoothly. There was squash, wild onions, cabbage and cactus, which actually tasted surprisingly good. It was like eating asparagus. For dessert, we ate something that looked a lot like pumpkin pie. It was pretty good too. For the remainder of the meal, the sheriff and the chief talked about the hardships of Native Americans who were forced to live on reservations. The sheriff appeared sympathetic, and everything I had learned about this man told me he was very sincere. When it appeared our visit had come to an end, I leaned over to the sheriff and whispered.

"What about Abby and Tommy? Can we find out if they're here? Some people think they might be."

"Yeah, the crackpots," the sheriff said.

"Lone Wolf, what is the problem?" the chief asked.

"Chief, maybe you can help us. A few days ago, a brother and sister disappeared from a farm about thirty miles north of here. We're afraid they might have been kidnapped."

"And you want to know if they are here?" the chief asked.

"I've told people they're crazy to think that the

Cheyenne tribe is behind it, but if you might have heard or seen anything, we'd really appreciate it."

The chief clapped his hands. The women who had brought in the food reappeared. He spoke to them in Cheyenne. They exited, and moments later another man entered the teepee. He nodded to us. The chief said something to him, and the man shook his head.

"Sheriff," the man said. "I can assure you that our people are not behind this terrible act. If you'd like, you can search the entire reservation. But I guarantee you will find nothing."

"I believe you, Wounded Dove," the sheriff said. "There's no need for a search." He paused. "Have you heard or seen anything about two missing white children?"

"No, I'm sorry, I haven't," he said.

"Well, thank you. That narrows things a little."

The sheriff and the chief said their goodbyes and we left the teepee. We climbed back onto the buckboard as Fallen Oak appeared. He bowed to the sheriff and shook his hand. He was now in his regular Cheyenne clothing, but still holding the clothes I had given him. He handed them to me. On the top was the magnet I had been carrying around in my pocket.

"What's that?" the sheriff said. He picked it up and ran his finger across it. "I've never seen anything like this."

"It's a magnet," I said.

"A magnet," the sheriff said. "I've heard of those, but I've never seen one so smooth."

I slid it into my pocket. "I doubt if there's any need for these around here."

As we made our way out of the camp, many of the tribespeople smiled and waved to us. I tried waving back. I had a really good feeling about having come here. The sheriff and Doc had done a wonderful thing. It was nice to see that some folks living in this time were genuinely kind to the Native Americans. But, as history tells us, that was not the sentiment held by most Americans in the 1800s.

When we exited the reservation, we passed through the burial grounds one more time. It was hard not to stare at the bodies on top of those scaffolds. I understood why the Cheyenne people chose not to bury their dead in the ground, but it was still a little weird having those bodies out there where anyone could mess with them. As we traveled in the direction of Abilene, I wondered what kind of reception would be waiting for the sheriff when we got back to town. After all, if they hadn't figured it out by now, they would soon learn that he had deceived them. The Scarlett Fever ploy was genius, but there would be a lot of folks who would be angry about it.

"Sheriff, do you think people in town will be upset when they figure out how we tricked them and took the boy back to the reservation?"

"*We* didn't trick them. *I* did. You have nothing to worry about."

"We're in this together," I said. "Good or bad."

He put his arm around me. "Spoken like a loyal deputy sheriff." He smiled.

Now that one crisis had been averted, I wondered if he would consider changing course and heading to the Kimball ranch to look for the kids.

"Sheriff, I was wondering about one more thing."

"Why do I have the feeling I know what you're about to ask?" he said.

"'Cause maybe you were thinking the same thing?"

"I was, Pete." With a straight face, "We should head

back to Abilene..." Then with a smile, "...by way of the Kimball ranch."

"Great. I know you won't be sorry. I have a good feeling about this. I think the kids are there somewhere."

"Well, I hope you're right. I really do."

We pushed the horses hard as we began what I hoped would be a successful rescue mission. While we were talking and eating with the chief, we later learned that some of the women at the reservation had rubbed down our horses, fed them, and gave them water. Since we had to cover some rough terrain, that, let me tell you, was a real blessing. As we traveled, I took the time to get to know the sheriff a little better.

"Sheriff, can I ask you a personal question?"

"Fire away."

"How come you never married?"

He stopped the buckboard and folded his arms. "Now how would you know about that unless you were trying to mess with the future. Remember what I told you about that?"

"Honest, sheriff, I'm not trying to mess with anything. It's just that I've read a lot about you, but I never saw anything in any of those books that said you ever got married."

"Pete, I'm afraid that news is downright disappointing. I had always considered settling down and getting married *after* I retired from sheriffing. But apparently that doesn't happen. I wish you had never told me."

I felt bad—really bad. Now I knew why the sheriff didn't want me telling him anything about how things turned out in the future. The reason, of course, why Amos Malone never took a wife in retirement is because he never reached retirement. His life ended while he was still on the job. But how could I tell him that? Then he'd really be depressed.

He put his hand on my shoulder. "I'm sorry. That wasn't fair. You were just asking a question." He smiled. "So, you wanted to know why I never got married. Does engaged count?"

"I'm not sure. When was that?"

"A long time ago. Before I decided to make law enforcement a full-time profession."

"You still haven't told me why you never got married?"

"It's a long story." He sighed. He flicked the reins and we were back on our way. "I was a deputy in Abilene working for Sheriff Hannibal Bass some thirty years ago. I had gotten to know the sheriff's family really well, especially his wife, Sophie. One day the sheriff was headed to the capital on business. He asked me to keep an eye on his wife and children. I had dinner with them a couple of times while he was gone. One night after his boys went to bed, Sophie opened up. She knew I was engaged at the time. She asked me to consider breaking off the engagement. I didn't know what she was talking about. She then told me what it was like being married to a lawman. When he left the house in the morning, you wondered if that would be the last time you would ever see him. Then you were a nervous wreck all day worrying about him. When he finally walked through that door at night, you looked to the heavens and you thanked God he was still alive. 'You don't want to put a woman through that kind of torture each day, now do you? It's just wouldn't be fair to her.'"

"The more I thought about it, the more I realized she was right. And I swore from that moment on that I would never do that to a woman I loved. I couldn't go to work each day and leave a woman behind who feared for my safety every minute. It was no kind of life. The next day I broke off my engagement."

"Oh, I see." But I really didn't. It just didn't seem fair that a man would have to deny himself a wife because his job was too dangerous. I understood the sheriff's reasoning, but I bet there were a lot of women out there who would gladly marry this man despite the perils of his job. But Amos Malone was too unselfish to put a wife through that misery. I felt bad for him but I respected his decision. It was amazing, I thought, what you learn about people when you have a chance to talk to them in person. None of the books on Sheriff Amos *Lone Wolf* Malone had ever mentioned anything about him deciding not to get married.

"So, what ever happened to her?" I asked.

"To who?"

"The girl you were engaged to."

He looked forward at the horizon and stared wistfully. "Marian. Marian Couture. Her father was French Canadian. Well, let me tell you. Marian was none too happy about my decision. She tried to talk me out of it. Said she wasn't like other women. Said she could handle being married to a lawman. But I was young and stubborn and proud. Once I made my mind up, there was no goin' back."

"Is she still in Abilene?"

"She is. She runs the dress shop in town."

"Did she ever get married?"

He shook his head. "And I couldn't figure it out. She was a very pretty gal. Still is. Could have had a bunch of suitors if she wanted. I think about her sometimes, but then I look down and see that star on my chest, and I know it's not meant to be. Oh, well, that's life, I guess."

I couldn't stop thinking about how the sheriff had plans to court a lady and settle down with her after retirement—a retirement that would never happen. Unless, of course, I were to break my promise and tell him about that card game. The sheriff was so stubborn about not wanting to know anything about his future. I wanted to respect his wishes, but I also wanted to see him stick around long enough to enjoy a happy and healthy retirement. I wrestled with the decision of what to do. I only hoped I'd know before it was too late.

CHAPTER 18

THE SHERIFF AND I MADE SMALL TALK FOR THE NEXT FEW miles. Eventually we found our way to the Kimball ranch. Like before when we passed the corral, we saw cowboys busting broncos. We pulled up in front of the main house and got out. A man who was sitting on the fence jumped off and walked over. He was in a dirty shirt and chaps. He had, no doubt, done ten rounds with one of the wild horses.

"Yeah, what do you want?" he said.

"I'm Sheriff Amos Malone from Abilene. Is Mr. Kimball in?"

"No, he and his wife are out of town on business. Won't be back till tomorrow."

"Is his son, Fred, around by any chance?"

"Yeah, I think he's in the house," the cowboy said. "Why?"

"Would you mind getting him for me?"

"What's this all about anyway?"

"Well, it's a private matter," the sheriff said.

"I don't think Mr. Kimball would like you talking to his son when he's not here."

"I think it'll be okay."

"Maybe we should send someone to get him. You can wait right here."

"Wait around here for hours?!" the sheriff said. "I don't think so. Just go in the house and get the boy for us."

"And if I don't want to?"

Sheriff Malone chuckled. "You're interfering with an ongoing investigation. That's a jailable offense. If you want to spend a few nights behind bars, be my guest. But I think you'll do the right thing."

The man made a face and headed for the house. Moments later, Fred appeared.

"Yeah," Fred said.

Yeah? Is that any way to speak to a member of law enforcement? This kid was a real prize.

"Young man, I have a few questions for you about the disappearance of Abby and Tommy Walker."

"Like I told your *friend*, I don't know nothing about that."

"We have an eyewitness who puts you with the two of them moments before they went missing."

"He's a liar."

"And we found a doll owned by Abby Walker on the outskirts of this ranch. This was a doll that Abby never let out of her sight. Meaning that she was in this vicinity a short time ago. And there was no reason for her to be anywhere around here unless she was brought here against her will."

"That's a lot of fancy talk that don't mean nothing to me. Listen, I got work to do. Are you finished?"

"I've just begun. I want you and all ranch personnel to stay right here while I search this property."

"You got no right to do that."

"I got every right to do so." He turned to me. "C'mon, Pete, let's start in the house."

"You can't go in there. My parents aren't home."

"How about you tell them about it when they get back."

I followed the sheriff up to the front door. Fred was still yelling something. We ignored him and entered the premises.

"You look upstairs and I'll search down here," the sheriff said. "And look everywhere—in closets, under beds, behind vanities—everywhere. Keep your eyes open for trap doors. Most of these places have them."

"Got it." I ran upstairs and poked my head into one of the bedrooms.

This was a really big house. The Kimballs must be loaded, I thought. I dropped down and checked under the bed. Then in the closet and behind the dresser. No one here. I did that with the next five bedrooms. I couldn't find hide nor hair of either of the missing kids. Before I went back downstairs, I checked a couple of hall closets. But again, no sign of them. I was just about to head down to the first floor when I spotted what looked like some kind of compartment in the ceiling. Of course, the attic. It would be the perfect place to hide someone.

There was a handle on the compartment door. I jumped up and pulled it down. When I did so, a ladder opened up and extended to the floor. I decided to climb up and check things out. When I got up there, I was happy to see a window in the corner that pretty much lit up the area. I looked for any signs of life. When I had pretty much searched the entire attic area, I spotted something out of the corner of my eye. It was a face. The face of a girl. Could it be Abby? I was almost afraid to look. And then I realized it was just a doll—a doll's head actually. Pretty soon, I realized the floor was covered with various doll parts—heads, legs, arms, torsos, etc. I had no idea what they were doing here but since it had nothing to do with the missing kids, they were of no interest to me. I went downstairs to rejoin the sheriff. When I found him, he was in the food pantry.

"Anything?" I said.

"Nothing. What about you?"

I shook my head.

"And you're sure you looked everywhere?"

"I scoured the upstairs, top to bottom. Even the attic. There's no sign of them."

"Let's go out and check the barn," he said. "It's the only other place to look."

I followed the sheriff out the front door and over to the barn. A few of the ranch hands were blocking the entrance.

"There's nothing here," one of them said.

"Well, now that makes me even more interested. Get out of my way, fellas. I need to get in there," the sheriff said.

The men were forming a human wall. There was no way around them.

"Gentlemen, I explained to one of your crew a few minutes ago that interfering with an ongoing investigation is against the law. Either move or face arrest."

They didn't budge. Instead of drawing his gun, the sheriff instead pulled a set of handcuffs from his belt and approached the ranch hand closest to him.

"Turn around and put your hands behind your back."

Again, no movement. The sheriff grabbed the man by the arm and spun him around. He slapped a cuff on one of his wrists and was about to do so with the other one when the man threw his arms in the air.

"All right, all right," he said.

I wasn't sure what I would have done if the men had jumped the sheriff. I was thankful it hadn't come to that. But once again, Sheriff Malone had gotten the job done without resorting to gunplay. Some of the ranch hands were a little bent out of shape, but everyone was still alive, and that was the important thing.

The sheriff pointed to the hayloft as we walked into the barn. "Pete, you wanna look up there, and I'll start down here."

The ranch hands were still standing in the doorway watching our every move. I walked up to a ladder and began my climb to the hayloft. When I got up there, all I found was hay—some loose and some in bales. I walked around kicking the hay to and fro, hoping that something or someone might be hidden underneath. Within a couple of minutes, I was certain there was no one up there. I climbed back down the ladder and hooked up with the sheriff.

"The hay loft is empty," I said.

"There's nothing down here either." The sheriff pounded on a post. "Where the heck are those kids?! They couldn't have just vanished." He took off his hat and pounded it on the side of his leg. "What are we missing?"

I shrugged.

"I'm at a loss, Pete. I don't know where else to look." He sighed. "Let's head back to town and talk about our next move, whatever that is."

I felt the same way. "I was so sure Fred Kimball had something to do with the disappearance of the kids that I stopped considering other possibilities."

"I'm not sure there are any other possibilities."

I followed the sheriff out of the barn and over to our horses. On our way there, we met a cocky Fred Kimball.

"Told ya. Told ya they're not here," he said.

"And why were you so sure they weren't? Could it be because you know where they are?" the sheriff said.

"I don't know what you're talking about," Fred said. He seemed defensive.

"I got a good notion to cuff you right here and drag your sorry butt to jail. Maybe then you'll feel like talking."

Fred went white as a sheet. There was no way he expected to be arrested. If the sheriff kept the pressure on, he just might crack.

"You can't take me in. I ain't done nothin'."

The sheriff walked up to Fred and stuck his finger in his chest. "One thing I know for sure, Kimball, is that you're too dumb to have pulled this off alone."

"What are you talking about?! I just—" He stopped in mid-sentence. He was just about to spill his guts but he caught himself. That may have been our best chance to trick him into a confession.

"My parents are gonna hear about this," he said.

A few of the ranch hands appeared.

"Well, you can tell the boy's parents they can pick him up in jail," the sheriff said. "C'mon, Fred, let's go."

"No, you can't do this. I didn't do anything. It wasn't my idea."

Keep talking, Fred. With each statement, he was getting closer and closer to admitting his involvement.

"I'm not gonna say anything else. And you can't make me." The ranch hands had now surrounded him.

I didn't think the sheriff was serious about arresting him with so little physical evidence. We had to keep him talking. Eventually he would put his foot completely into his mouth and we'd have what we'd need to bring him in. The Sampson kids had made a less than positive ID. I knew that. The sheriff knew that. But Fred didn't know that.

"Sounds like you're on a fishing expedition, Sheriff," one of the ranch hands said. "You ain't got no proof the boy was involved. I think it's time for you to go."

"No proof?! The boy as much as admitted it a minute ago."

"He was confused. You tricked him. Freddie gets himself into an occasional scrape, but he ain't a bad kid. Why don't you come back when the boy's parents are here?"

"You can count on that," the sheriff said. He hopped onto his horse. I did the same. A moment later, we rode off.

The sheriff was mum until we got to the main road. "We almost had him back there."

"Well, at least, we now know he was involved."

"I guarantee that. But there's got to be someone else pulling the strings. Freddie's not bright enough to have called the shots. He's covering for someone, that's for sure."

"But who? Who would do such a thing?" I asked.

"I just don't know, Pete. I just don't know." He sighed. "How about if we head back to town, have dinner, get a good night's sleep, and head back out tomorrow morning.

Then we'll be refreshed, and we might see something we've been missing."

"I hate to quit, Sheriff."

"I know, but it's time to regroup and rethink this thing."

"I hate to say it but each day that passes makes me think we'll never find those kids. If we're wrong about someone in the area kidnapping them, then it's possible they could be miles from here by now."

"You're absolutely right, Pete. I've thought of that. And if that's the case, then they could be completely out of the Abilene jurisdiction. Then we'd have to turn over the case to another lawman. I just want to be sure they're not hiding right here under our noses before we assume they're out of the area. Okay?"

"I guess so."

"C'mon, let's head back. Who knows? When we wake up tomorrow morning, we may have figured this whole thing out."

I nodded. But what if we couldn't figure it out? What if we never figured it out? What if we never found the Walker kids? What could have happened to them? I shook my head. It was just too painful to think about. We were close—closer than we had ever been before. But had we run out of time? More importantly, had those kids run out of time?

CHAPTER 19

WHEN WE GOT BACK TO TOWN, WE WENT STRAIGHT TO dinner. We found Doc at Halsey's sitting alone so we decided to join him.

"Amos, any news on those children?" Doc asked.

"Unfortunately, no. And we're running out of leads."

"Well, it's a shame—a real shame. How are the parents holding up?"

"To be honest, we haven't talked to them in a few days." The sheriff turned toward me. "Pete, maybe that's where we'll start tomorrow morning. We'll head to the Walker farm. What do you think?"

"I like the idea. Maybe they'll remember something they had forgotten to tell us."

"You never know," Doc said. "When people are coping with a tragedy, they don't think straight. Maybe they'll recall something."

The sheriff looked over at Doc's plate with a curious expression. "What are you eating?"

Doc rolled his eyes. "The worst item on the menu—catfish stew. It's all they've got right now."

The sheriff made a face. "I've got some jerky in the office. It can't be any worse than that."

I heard a commotion near the door. The hostess seemed to be having a problem with a group of people who had just walked in. They were arguing about something, but I couldn't hear what they were saying. A moment later, they were standing around our table and hovering over us.

"Sheriff, you know me. I'm the President of the Abilene Chamber of Commerce. I have come here to tell you that many of our members are quite upset with what you did. That was a dirty trick you pulled on us," he said.

"Dirty trick?" the sheriff said. "I don't follow."

"You know darn well what I'm talking about. Bringing that Injun to Doc's office and then sneaking him out. Those people are bad for business. They don't belong in our town. They're savages, and we don't want them here."

"Is that right?"

"Yeah, in my book, the only good Injun is a dead Injun."

The sheriff stood. "And that's why I snuck him out. If any of your *members* had harmed that boy, I'd have to throw them in jail. Is that what you would have wanted?"

"All we wanted was to string up that Injun."

"Listen, Jonathan, the *savages* you're talking about are human beings, the same as you and me. They were created in God's image and likeness, just like the rest of us." He picked up his spoon. "Now I'm trying to eat my dinner. Can we have this conversation at another time?"

"You know, Sheriff," he said, "there's a lot of people in this town who aren't very happy with what you did. Now don't get me wrong. You've done a great job cleaning up the streets of Abilene since you've been here. It's a safe place now for women and children. But your position on the Indian situation is simply unacceptable. And people don't like it."

"They'll get over it," the sheriff said.

"I don't think so. Those people are about to take the matter into their own hands. I didn't want to tell you this but there's a petition going around town to have you replaced. Once we have enough signatures, we're gonna send it to the governor. And then maybe we'll get ourselves a sheriff who ain't no bleedin' heart Injun lover."

The sheriff smiled. "Jonathan, be my guest. Governor Harrington already has it in for me. This might tip the scales in your favor. There's nothing I can do about it. I just have to follow my conscience and hope that people agree with my decisions."

"Well, there's a bunch o' people in this town who don't agree with you. Your days here are numbered."

"All I can do is hope that the good people of Abilene—and I mean the *good* people—refuse to sign your petition."

"That ain't gonna happen, Sheriff. So, you better start packin' now."

The sheriff shrugged. "If you can convince the governor to get rid of me, more power to you. And if it happens, I would more than welcome an early retirement."

"So would we," the man said. The group turned and headed out the door.

"Sheriff, what did you mean the governor *already has it in for you?*" I asked.

The sheriff sat back in his chair and smiled. "The current governor of Kansas is a fellow named John Martin, and Governor Martin is no friend of the Indian. If he had his way, the reservations would be smaller, and the penalties of leaving them would be more strict. I've been warned on more than one occasion to back off my present stance, and as he puts it, *'embrace the will of the people.'*"

"Pete, here's the crazy thing," Doc Conrad said. "For a town of its size, Abilene has one of the lowest crime rates in the state. And that's all because of your boss here."

"Isn't that important to the governor?" I asked.

"There's only thing important to this governor— votes."

"Amos, if this petition gets any steam, it's not gonna be too pleasant around here for you," Doc said. "If you've got any vacation time left, maybe you oughta go fishin' for a couple of weeks. By then this whole thing may blow over."

"I'm not runnin', Doc. If they want to get rid of me, let 'em try."

"I can't believe this," I said. "With all the good you've done for this town, how can one incident make them forget all of that? It's just not right."

"Pete, I appreciate the support, but this is something you gotta get used to. When folks get all up in arms over something, all that matters is how you handled that particular problem for them. It doesn't matter how you've done things for the last twenty or thirty years."

"Then these people sure have a short memory," I said.

"Amen to that," Doc chimed in.

"By the way, Doc, thanks for everything you did for Fallen Oak," the sheriff said. "You didn't have to stick your neck out the way you did. I'm sorry to have put you in that position."

Doc smiled. "It was the right thing to do. You don't need to apologize."

"It sounds like that bunch wasn't too happy when they found out we had all snuck out of your office."

"That would be an understatement. They accused me of being part of some conspiracy. At one point, they threatened to burn me down. But I knew they weren't serious. I just let them blow off some steam. Within a few minutes, they were all gone."

"Well, I'm sure glad to hear that," the sheriff said.

"It was a really brave thing you and the sheriff did, Doc," I said. "I couldn't be any prouder to call you my friends."

Doc reached over and put his hand on my shoulder. "And I'm just as happy to have you as my friend, Pete. I think we all work together really well if you ask me." He winked.

"So, partner, you up for some catfish stew?" the sheriff asked.

I grinned. "That doesn't sound too appetizing."

"It isn't," Doc said.

"How about if we skip dinner and go straight to the dessert," I said.

The sheriff and Doc laughed.

"I couldn't agree more," the sheriff said. He motioned to the waiter. "Hey, Max, can we get a dessert menu over here."

A few minutes later, we had made our choice—apple pie à la mode. It was delish. After dinner, we walked Doc back to his office and returned to the jail. We didn't talk much. We had struck out at Fred Kimball's and didn't have any idea what our next move might be. Since we were fairly tired, having gotten up in the middle of the night to return Fallen Oak to the reservation, we drifted off rather quickly.

The next morning, we woke, got cleaned up, visited Halsey's for breakfast, and were on our way to the

Walker farm by seven thirty. The sheriff was fairly quiet during the ride. I knew he was trying to figure out this mystery, but nothing was popping into either of our heads. He also had to be concerned about the petition to have him thrown out of his job. I wasn't sure how he could concentrate on the missing kids with that hanging over his head.

I was worried for him, but I was also worried about finding Abby and Tommy. I was so sure we would have found something at the Kimball ranch. I couldn't believe we hadn't. I was left with an empty feeling. I was starting to forget what Abby looked like. It had been nearly ten days since she and Tommy had disappeared and we had little to show for our investigation.

"Do you think the Walkers will be upset that we haven't turned up anything yet?" I said.

"I'd be upset if I were them. They have every right to be disappointed in us—well, in me, at least."

"In me too, Sheriff. I have nothing to show for the last few days."

"You're very loyal, Pete. But people don't expect *you* to solve this case. They expect *me* to. Heck, it's my job. It's why the town hired me." He seemed to think to himself for a moment. "You know, maybe it wouldn't be such a bad thing if the governor did let me go. Then maybe they can get some younger blood in here and get some results."

"Don't say that! You're the best sheriff in the territory. In the state of Kansas. These folks would be lost without you. Then again, if they did hire a new sheriff, they might find out just how valuable you were. And they'd be begging you to come back."

He smiled. "That's nice to hear, but I can't see a lot of these folks ever admitting they were wrong. If they were unhappy with a new sheriff, they'd keep their mouths shut."

We could just about make out the Walker farm in the distance. We rode for a few more minutes when we spotted Mr. Walker in the fields. When he saw us, he waved and joined us in the farmyard.

"Do you have any news for us, Sheriff?" Mr. Walker said frantically.

"We're making some progress, Hiram, but we haven't found the kids yet. I'm sorry."

"But you're getting closer?"

"Yes, we're getting closer. I hope to have some news in the next week." The sheriff looked at me with an expression suggesting he had just lied.

But who could blame him? We had to give these people some hope, any kind of hope, even if it wasn't exactly true. By this time, Mrs. Walker had come out of the house. It was hard to believe it was the same woman. Her face was pale and thin. For that matter, her whole body was thinner. This woman couldn't have eaten much in the last week and a half. If we didn't find these kids soon, she might just waste away.

"Hello, Sheriff," she said. "I take it you don't have good news for us."

"They're getting closer, Martha," her husband said.

"I've started to give up," she said. "I don't think we'll ever see them again."

Mr. Walker walked over and hugged his wife. "Don't say that. Why don't you go back in the house and lie down while I talk to the sheriff." He walked her to the door.

The sheriff and I got off our horses and waited for Mr. Walker to return. A moment later, he rejoined us.

"Sheriff, you just have to find our children. If you

don't, I'll be a widower for sure. A little piece of Martha dies off each day the kids are missing."

"I'm really sorry to see the toll this is taking on your wife," the sheriff said. "Hiram, we're doing everything we can. We've talked to dozens of folks. We even searched a ranch yesterday where we thought the children might have been hidden."

"We're following up on every lead, Mr. Walker," I said. "I know I speak for the sheriff when I say that we won't rest until we've brought Abby and Tommy home to you. That's a promise."

Mr. Walker managed a half-smile. "He's a good boy, Amos. You've taught him well."

The sheriff smiled at me. "Hiram, can you think of any detail that you haven't already told us that might help in our search?"

Mr. Walker sat down on a barrel next to a horse trough. He looked tired. "I just can't think of anything else. Martha and I have been racking our brains trying to come up with that one piece of information that will help, but we keep coming up dry."

"Well, don't worry about it. We'll work with what we have. You just take care of your wife. Don't let her give up hope."

"Something will break soon," I said. "I just know it. We're so close, I can taste it."

"I hope you're right, son," he said. "I really do."

Suddenly, out of nowhere, Killer, the three-legged family dog, came running up to me. I put my hand out carefully. I still wasn't completely sure how he felt about me. He proceeded to sniff my hand and then began to lick it. The entire time his tail was wagging. I crouched down to pet him.

"He remembers you," Mr. Walker said. He turned to the sheriff. "Killer and I have searched the entire area around the farm. I keep hoping he'll pick up the scent. That rainstorm the day after the children went missing washed away any tracks we might have found. And it seemed to have done the same thing with the scent. I know that if Abby is anywhere near here, Killer would have found her by now. And that's why I'm worried the kids are a long way from here."

"That may not be the case," the sheriff said. "We still have plenty of places to search in the area."

Mr. Walker let out a loud, long sigh. "You know, Amos, Martha has just about given up any hope of ever seeing our children again. Now she just prays that the person who took them will hopefully treat them well."

The sheriff seemed to be at a loss for words. He just stared at the ground.

Mr. Walker shook his head. "I just hope no one's hurt them—or worse."

"Hiram, you gotta have faith. We've put the word out all over the territory that if anyone sees the kids or anything suspicious, they are to get that information to our office as soon as possible. We have a lot of eyes out there."

"Well, I best tend to my wife. Thanks for stopping by." Mr. Walker turned and headed back to the house.

We jumped back onto our horses and walked them over to a water trough where they drank. We then headed out toward the prairie. Killer followed us until we made it to the main road. Then he barked a couple of times and headed back home.

"I thought it would be a good idea to come out here, Sheriff, but all it did was make me feel even worse," I said.

"I know what you mean, Pete. I feel awful for that family. I just don't know where else to look. If you get any brainstorms, I'd sure welcome them."

But I didn't have any brainstorms. I had nothing. And I knew time was running out. We had played the Fred Kimball card, but it didn't get us any closer to finding the kids. I was sure he was somehow involved but he had clammed up. We wouldn't be getting any more information out of him. Once his parents found out we had searched their home, I doubted if they would ever let us talk to him again.

I followed the sheriff as we made our way back to town. I guessed we would head back to the office and try to plot out our next move, whatever that might be. I pulled the map from my shirt pocket and glanced at it. We had visited just about all of Abby's and Tommy's friends. When I spotted an X on the map where we hadn't gone yet, I wondered if I should bring it to the sheriff's attention. I wasn't sure if he would want to visit a family that would probably leave us no closer to finding the kids. But then I thought—what the heck. How could it hurt?

"Sheriff, there's one more family on the map who we haven't visited yet."

"Who's that?"

"It says Johnny Pearson under the X."

"Yeah, the Pearsons. They're pig farmers."

"It seems to be on our way. What do you say?"

The sheriff shrugged. "Pete, I think we'd just be wasting our time. None of these families have gotten us any closer to solving this crime."

"Well, the Sampson kids did point us in the direction of Fred Kimball."

"But I thought you said they weren't able to identify him."

"Yeah, but who knows? Maybe the Pearsons are the missing link. Maybe they know something no one else knows."

"And maybe they don't."

We went back and forth for a couple more minutes before the sheriff finally gave in.

"All right, but since this is your idea, you do the interview."

"I don't mind," I said.

The sheriff reluctantly turned his horse in the direction of the Pearson farm. I knew he had only agreed to go as a favor to me. I only hoped I hadn't let him down. Another dead end was the last thing we needed right now.

CHAPTER 20

IT ONLY TOOK US ABOUT FIFTEEN MINUTES TO GET TO THE Pearson farm. As we got closer, we knew it was the right place by the sound and smell of hogs. It was unmistakable. I couldn't imagine waking up to those sounds and that stench every morning. I wondered how long it took to get that smell off your clothes. I glanced at the sheriff and pinched my nose.

"This is your idea, remember," he said.

I smiled. I was praying it would pay off. We rode up to the farmhouse and tied the horses to the front banister. Soon, a woman who was fixing the back of her hair, came out the front door.

"Sheriff Malone, what a nice surprise," she said.

The sheriff extended his hand. "Hilda, so nice to see you. I hope all is well with you and your family."

She untied her apron and tossed it over a clothesline. "Can't complain. God's been good to us." She looked in my direction and smiled.

"This is my new apprentice, Pete Moss," the sheriff said.

The woman held out her hand. "Nice to meet you, son. So, Sheriff, what brings you out here?"

A man in a checkered shirt and overalls came out of the barn.

"Hilda, I suppose you've heard about the disappearance of Abby and Tommy Walker," the sheriff said.

She grabbed the sides of her head. "When I heard about it, I nearly fainted. I just couldn't believe it."

"Howdy, Sheriff," the man said.

"Hi, Jed, how are you?"

"Doing fine, thanks."

"By the way, this is my new deputy, Pete."

"How do, Pete," he said.

"Nice to meet you, sir."

"Jed, I was just telling Hilda that we're still trying to find any clues that might lead us to the Walker children. They disappeared nearly two weeks ago."

The man shook his head. "I pray every day that those youngins will show up unharmed. Have you made any progress?"

"Very little, I'm afraid."

"I visited Martha a couple of days ago," Mrs. Pearson said. "I brought her some cinnamon rolls. She didn't look good. I'm really worried about her."

"We just came from there," the sheriff said. "She's gotten very frail. I'm gonna ask Doc Conrad to pay her a visit."

"I think that would be a good idea," she said.

The sheriff nodded in my direction. I knew it was my cue to conduct the interview.

"Mr. and Mrs. Pearson, is there any chance we could talk to Johnny? I know he's one of Tommy's friends."

Mr. Pearson glanced at his wife. "Where is that boy?"

"He's in his bedroom reading," she said. "I'll go get him."

We waited a minute for Johnny to join us. A small boy in a white teeshirt and jeans soon appeared.

"Johnny," his mother said, "this is Sheriff Malone and his deputy, Pete. They have some questions for you."

"What kind of questions?"

"About Tommy Walker," she said.

"Have they found Tommy yet?" he asked.

"No, Johnny," I said. "That's why we wanted to talk to you. We need to find out if you saw him or spoke to him lately."

The boy shook his head. "No, sorry."

"Can you remember the last time you saw him?"

"Not really."

"Do you recall what you talked about when you did see him?"

He looked up at his mother. "I don't remember, Mom."

"That's okay," she said. "Just tell this nice young man anything you remember about the last time you played with Tommy."

Johnny thought to himself. "I think we played mumblety-peg. We used the old stump behind Tommy's house."

"And do you remember when that might have been?"

He shook his head. This was going nowhere. None of this information was helpful. I glanced at the sheriff. His expression suggested he thought we were wasting our time. Before I could ask another question, there was the sound of a horse coming from the road leading into the farm. When I looked up, I spotted a buckboard heading in our direction. A moment later, I could recognize the person at the reins. It was Mrs. Hailey. What was she doing here anyway? I was in the middle of a serious interrogation. I noticed that Johnny ran over to his mother and held onto her tightly when he saw Mrs. Hailey.

"I don't want to go with her," he said. "I don't like her."

Mrs. Hailey was now within earshot. "Hello, Pearsons," she yelled out. "Would Johnny like to join me for a ride today?"

"No, I don't think so," Mrs. Pearson said. "We're visiting with the sheriff right now."

"I can wait," Mrs. Hailey said.

I needed to do something. It was clear Johnny wanted nothing to do with this woman. I had to come to his aid.

"I'm afraid this is going to take quite some time, ma'am," I said. "We plan to be here for the better part of the afternoon."

Her expression suddenly changed. Her eyes narrowed. She didn't seem happy with me.

"All right, maybe some other time," she said. She was now glaring at me. She pulled the reins, turned the buckboard around, and left in a hurry.

When Mrs. Hailey was far enough away, Mrs. Pearson crouched down to Johnny's level.

"You will never ever have to go anywhere with that woman. Okay?"

He nodded.

She turned to us. "I can't put my finger on it but there's just something about that woman that isn't right. I wish she would just leave the children alone. I know she lost a daughter many years ago, but I'm just not willing to share my child with her. I'm sorry."

And suddenly I had the brainstorm I had been waiting for. Of course, of course. Why hadn't I thought of it before? It all made perfect sense. How could I have been so dense?

"Sheriff, I think we're done here with Johnny. I've learned everything I need to. Are you ready to go?"

The sheriff gave me a funny look. He had to be wondering why I was in such a hurry all of the sudden. I would explain everything to him as soon as we were off the farm. We had to get going as soon as possible.

"Thank you, Mr. and Mrs. Pearson," I said. "And thank you, Johnny. You were a big help."

I walked over to Shuffle and hopped on board. The sheriff was still standing in the middle of the farmyard. He shrugged as he walked over to his horse.

"Jed, Hilda, thanks much. If either of you happen to see anything unusual, please let me know."

"We will, Sheriff," Mr. Pearson said.

"So long, fellas," Mrs. Pearson said.

We headed up the path in the direction of the main road. When I knew we couldn't be overheard, I pulled on the reins and stopped Shuffle.

"What was that all about back there?" the sheriff asked. "You were in the middle of an interview, and then you just stopped. I had a few more questions for the boy. What's going on?"

"Sheriff, I know where Abby and Tommy are."

"What?"

"I don't know why I hadn't thought of it before."

"What are you talking about?"

"It was Mrs. Hailey. She was the one who took the kids. Don't you see. You heard what Mrs. Pearson said about her losing a daughter. She wants children. And since she's too old to have her own, she just took someone else's kids."

"Pete, that sounds like a stretch."

"But it's not. I was with her at the General Store when she was trying to buy licorice root for Abby Walker. Then after the kids went missing, she was in the General Store again buying more licorice *for her houseguests*."

"Maybe the woman likes licorice root."

"But she doesn't. Don't you see? I heard her tell Mr. Crowley that she can't stand the stuff."

"Maybe she *does* have houseguests."

"Well, why don't you and I go over there and see for ourselves. The only houseguests we'll find there will be the Walker kids. I guarantee it."

"Oh, Pete, I don't know."

"Please, Sheriff!"

"What are we supposed to do—just waltz in there and tell her we want to search her property?"

"We can...we can tell her we're searching *all* the houses in the area. We can tell her we just got done searching the Pearson home. She might buy it."

The sheriff scratched the top of his head. "Explain this to me then. How does Fred Kimball fit into all of this?"

I paused. "I haven't figured out the connection yet—but there's gotta be one."

"This woman creeps out all the kids in the area. Wouldn't it make sense she might want one for herself?"

"I guess so. But is she capable of kidnapping? I agree she's a bit odd, but is she a criminal?"

"My money says she is. Please, Sheriff, can't we just go over there and see?"

He sighed. "All right, you've handled yourself like a real pro so far. I guess I owe you a chance to play out this hunch."

"Yessss!"

We headed in the direction of Mrs. Hailey's. It wouldn't take us more than a few minutes to get there. As we rode, I was imagining finding Abby and Tommy. I'd bet she has them tied up in an upstairs bedroom. And she's probably gagged them as well so no one could hear their screams. I'm going to enjoy carting this woman off to jail. A monster like that belongs behind bars. I could just picture the look on Abby's face when she realizes she's being rescued. I couldn't wait for it.

"There it is," the sheriff said.

In the distance was a small farmhouse surrounded by a wooden fence. Mrs. Hailey's buckboard was out front. There was a pretty good chance she was home. This was going to work out beautifully. We stopped the horses in the barnyard and dismounted. As we were walking up to the front door, Mrs. Hailey came out to greet us. But I wouldn't actually call it a *greeting*.

"Oh, it's you," she said, staring right at me.

"Mrs. Hailey, I wonder if we might have a minute," the sheriff said.

"I don't have a minute. I'm busy."

"It won't take long," he said.

"Sheriff, it's not a good time."

I could sense the desperation in her voice. She knew this was the end. There was no way she would allow us to search her home, but we weren't about to give her a choice.

"I assume you're aware that the Walker children have disappeared."

"Everyone knows that," she snapped.

"Well, we're just searching all the homes in the area looking for them."

"They ain't here," she said.

"We'd like to check for ourselves," the sheriff said.

"So, you're calling me a kidnapper *and* a liar. Is that it?"

Since this whole thing had been my idea. I thought it was about time for me to jump in.

"We're not accusing you of anything, Mrs. Hailey," I said. "We'd just like to have a look around. That's all."

She crossed her arms and smiled. "You think I'm hiding something, is that it?"

"No, ma'am," I said. "It's just routine." I waited for a response. There was none. "So, is it okay if we take a look?" I said.

"Be my guest."

I couldn't believe what I was hearing. I would have felt a lot better if she would have resisted. Then we would have known she was hiding something—or someone. But her willingness to let us search the house made me less confident we'd find anything. I was so sure about this. If I had screwed this up, it was pretty clear the sheriff wouldn't be open to any of my suggestions ever again.

Mrs. Hailey walked over to a front porch swing and sat down. "Just to show you I got nothing to hide, I'll sit right here while you tear the place apart."

The sheriff shook his head. "We're not gonna damage anything."

"Have at it then," she said.

The sheriff motioned for me to join him inside. We entered the premises and found ourselves in the living room. To the right was the kitchen, and to the left was a stairway that led to the second floor.

"Let's handle this like the Kimball search," the sheriff said. "You head upstairs. And, Pete, I hate to say it, but I don't have a very good feeling about this."

I didn't say a word. I was beginning to think he may be

right. I ran up the stairs to find two small bedrooms. This was nothing like the Kimball house. It would only take a few minutes to go through this entire place. Each room had a bed, a nightstand, and a dresser. Neither room had a closet. I looked all around, especially under the bed. I found nothing. I hustled over to the second bedroom and began that search. A minute later I was done. There was absolutely nothing here. I checked the ceiling. Maybe there was an attic. But there was none.

I was beginning to get a knot in the pit of my stomach. How could I have been so wrong about all of this? I couldn't believe the kids weren't here. I ran back downstairs to find the sheriff looking through the kitchen cabinets. He was on his knees. He glanced at me with a disgusted look on his face.

"Nothing. How about you?"

I shook my head.

"I think we owe this woman an apology," he said.

"I'll do it," I said. "It's my fault we're here."

"Well, don't do anything until we check the barn."

Of course, the barn. Maybe they were in there. We walked out the front door and noticed Mrs. Hailey still sitting on the swing.

"Convinced?" she said.

"We'd like to take a look in the barn," the sheriff said.

She shrugged. "Do your duty. But you're wasting your time."

The woman was so cool. Nothing seemed to bother her. This wasn't at all what I was expecting. We walked over to the barn. It smelled bad, but not as bad as the pig farm.

"You check the loft, Pete. I'll look down here."

I climbed up to the hayloft and found a lot of...hay. I

decided to look through it like I was searching for a hidden treasure. If those kids were up here, I was going to find them. But after ten minutes of tossing hay from one side of the loft to the other, I came to the realization that the Walker kids were nowhere to be seen. I had made a fool of myself—in front of Mrs. Hailey—and in front of the sheriff. I climbed down to the ground floor with egg on my face.

"I was afraid of this," the sheriff said.

I just stood there with a pained expression on my face.

"Don't worry about it. We all come up dry sometimes."

"I'm sorry, Sheriff. I'm sorry I dragged you over here. I'm sorry I put you through this."

He put his arm around me. "You know how many times my hunches have been wrong? Plenty. Let me tell you. It's part of the job. We learn from experiences like these. You'll be a better lawman tomorrow because of it."

We left the barn and walked up to the front porch. Mrs. Hailey was still seated on the swing. She had a smile on her face.

"I could have saved you gentlemen a lot of trouble," she said. "I told you those children weren't here. But you wouldn't listen."

I looked to the sheriff and then Mrs. Hailey. "I'm sorry we bothered you, ma'am. Please forgive us."

Her smile got wider. "You all done here, Sheriff?"

"We're done. We'll be heading out now." The sheriff walked over to his horse and hopped on.

I didn't say a word to him the entire ride back to Abilene. I could tell he wasn't in a particularly talkative mood. I sensed he was really disappointed about finding nothing at the Kimball ranch and the Hailey farm—two places I had been so sure about. With these two strikes against me, the sheriff had to be wondering if he'd made the right decision about bringing me back with him to 1888. He was looking for someone to take his place. He had to be thinking he'd have to stay in this job long past retirement age since I was hardly sheriff material. And I happened to be thinking the same thing. Maybe I was in way over my head. Maybe I had no business wearing a badge. I hadn't really earned it. I wondered if I'd ever earn it. Only time would tell. It was early July. The sheriff's fateful poker game was scheduled to be played on the eleventh. Time was running out.

CHAPTER 21

THE NEXT WEEK WAS MORE OF THE SAME. WE'D SIT AROUND and discuss the case. We'd go over every piece of evidence we had. We'd discuss possible suspects. We'd try to imagine where these kids could have been hidden. We'd head out to visit the friends of Abby and Tommy who we hadn't spoken to earlier. But none of those visits, however, amounted to much. We even checked the local bodies of water—streams and lakes—to make sure the kids hadn't gone swimming and drowned. That was a grim search. I was so glad we found nothing.

We soon realized we were out of suspects and out of evidence. There was just nowhere else to turn. I noticed that Sheriff Malone was getting more and more down as each day passed. And who could blame him? Everyone in town knew about the disappearance of the Walker kids, and everyone in town knew the sheriff had failed to locate the pair and reunite them with their parents.

We hadn't visited the Walkers for several days. We basically had no reason to. There was no news. Why should we drop in and get their hopes up? As the days passed, I watched the sheriff's appetite shrink. When we'd go over to Halsey's for a meal, he'd barely touch his food. Like me, Sheriff Malone had become obsessed with this case and our inability to find the missing kids. He started to talk about retiring early. He'd say he was getting older, and the town needed some new blood, younger blood, to help keep the peace. He was doubting himself left and right. I tried to give him occasional pep talks. Sometimes I would feel I had been able to motivate him. Other times, he would fall back into a state of depression.

I had spent so much time lately concentrating on the Walker case that I had almost forgotten about finding a way to warn the sheriff about the ill-fated poker game. I had completely lost track of time. When I stopped to figure out what the date was, I couldn't believe it.

"Sheriff, what's the date today?"

He checked a calendar on his desk. "It's July eleventh."

"July eleventh? It can't be. It just can't be."

"What's the problem? What's the big deal about July eleventh?"

I just sat there with my head in my hands. The sheriff could tell something was wrong.

"Oh," he said. "How stupid of me. It's one month since you first got here. Happy anniversary. I know I don't say it often enough, Pete, but I'm really glad you're here. I couldn't have made a better choice."

"It's not that, Sheriff. It's something else."

"What is it? What's bothering you?"

"I know you don't want me to go there, but I can't help it. I have to tell you what's going to happen today."

"Pete, I warned you."

"I know, I know, but it's really important. It's a matter of life and death."

"I don't want to hear it."

"Ohhh, you're so stubborn," I said.

"How many times do I have to tell you—we can't tamper with the future. If you were to tell me, and if I changed what I was going to do because of it, the lives of many other people—people we don't even know will be altered. And maybe altered in a bad way." He looked into my eyes. "You have to trust me. It's for the best. So, will you stop worrying about what's going to happen today, and just let it run its course?"

"But—"

"No buts. This conversation is over."

I dropped my head and sighed. I decided to let it go for the time being. I would just have to make an appearance at the saloon tonight during the poker game and warn him as the disgruntled gambler showed up. The sheriff may not feel this way now, but he would thank me when this was all over.

When I looked over, I caught the sheriff counting money on his desk.

"Someone's bail money?" I asked.

He smiled. "No, it's my poker winnings from last night. I had a really good game." He crouched down and opened the safe behind him. He placed the money inside and closed the safe door. "I have to remember to grab this money before the game tonight."

"I'm glad to hear you won big last night." I said.

"But I can't speak for everyone. There was this one fella—a stranger in town—who lost his shirt. I felt bad for him. He lost his whole bankroll. I decided to give him a couple of bucks for breakfast. After all, it's only money."

"Did he leave town, do you know?"

"I don't think so. I saw him walk over to the hotel about eleven."

"Do you expect him to show up for a game tonight?"

"I don't think so. One of the fellas said he was broke. Poor guy."

"You don't suppose he might return for some payback? Some people don't take kindly to losing." I needed to make the sheriff aware of the fact that this fellow could come back to get even. I wanted him to keep this in the back of his mind.

"I don't expect him to," the sheriff said.

"But what if he does? Will you be ready to defend yourself?"

"Pete, you worry too much. I make sure that I always take the seat at the table that faces the door. That way I can see trouble when it enters the saloon."

"Well, that's good. But what if that seat isn't available tonight?"

"I'd just ask one of the other players to switch with me."

"And what if he won't?"

"It's never happened. Why are you so interested in all of this?"

I wanted to tell him so badly about what was going to happen tonight during the game but I knew he'd never listen. Maybe I could just blurt it out quickly. Then he wouldn't have a chance to stop me. I decided to do it. After all, what did I have to lose?

I stood. "Sheriff, you can't play in that poker game tonight because—"

He put his hands over his ears and started yelling out gibberish so he couldn't hear what I was going to say.

When he was certain I had stopped speaking, he removed his hands.

"You sure do have a one-track mind, boy."

"I'm sorry. I couldn't help myself."

"Fight it, Pete. Fight it. You have to. It'll ruin everything."

"But what if it's a good thing. What if by telling you, I can—"

"Save my life?" he said.

I just stared at him. How did he know what I was going to say?

"Well, yeah," I said.

"It wouldn't matter. If my time on this earth is over, then it's over. It's been a good run. I have no regrets."

"Not even never settling down and getting married?"

He turned and looked out the window. He seemed to be thinking about something.

"That would be my one regret," he said. "But we don't always get what we want in life. It's just how it works." He smiled. "Now do me a favor—go walk around town and make sure everything's in order. I'm worried that the longer you sit here, the more likely it is you'll say something I don't want to hear."

I nodded. I grabbed my hat off the hook by the door and walked out onto Main Street. Since it was late morning, there was a healthy number of folks shopping and doing business in town. I walked down to the end of the street. I passed the hotel, the restaurant, the blacksmith's shop, Hugg's Grocery, the drugstore, the general store, the livery stable, Doc's office...wait a minute, Doc's office. Maybe he could help. Yeah, sure, they're good friends. They'd take advice from one another. What did I have to lose?

I knocked on the front door. When I heard a voice from inside, I walked in.

"Well, good morning, Pete. How are you this fine day?"

"Okay, I guess."

"Is something wrong?"

"I don't know exactly."

"Aren't you feeling well?" he asked.

"No, I'm fine. It's the sheriff."

"Is Amos sick?"

"Not really."

"Then what seems to be the problem?" he said.

I sat down. "Doc, can you do me a favor?"

"Why sure."

"Can you convince the sheriff not to play poker tonight?"

He smiled and crossed his arms. "Now that's an awfully strange request. What's it all about? Is the sheriff losing all his money?"

"No, he actually had a big win last night. It's just that I'm worried that something awful is going to happen to him if he plays tonight."

"Why would you say that?"

"No reason, I guess. I just have a bad feeling about it."

"Do you know something he doesn't?"

How do I answer that question without Doc finding out that I live a hundred-plus years in the future? It would almost be worth it to tell him why I was so certain about the event scheduled to take place tonight. If I told him the truth about how I got here, he'd have to believe me. Or he might not? It's possible he would think I was losing my mind. He might want to sedate me or confine me to his office until I began thinking more clearly. The more I thought about it, the more I realized I couldn't tell him the truth.

"I don't know of anything for sure. I just think something bad is gonna happen."

"Well, I can try to talk him out of joining the others tonight, but he really enjoys playing poker each evening. It relaxes him. And with the stress that comes with the kind of job he has, it's something I've encouraged him to do." Doc sighed. "I wish I knew more about this bad feeling you have."

I was beginning to realize the sheriff would be playing cards tonight, and there was nothing I could do about it. About all I *could* do is wait outside the saloon after dark, and when I see a character who looks threatening, I would yell to the sheriff to look out. It was my only option.

"I can't really explain it, Doc, but thanks anyway."

"I'll try to talk to him about it but if I can't give him a good enough reason not to play, I guarantee he's gonna be in that card game tonight."

"I know. Thanks again. I gotta go."

"Take care, son."

I left Doc's office and headed down Main Street. There was nothing more I could do now to save the sheriff's life. He refused to take my warnings and wouldn't let me tell him the truth about what was actually going to happen tonight. He didn't want me to alter the future in any way— even if it meant helping him avoid an untimely demise. I guess I'd have to wait until tonight during the actual poker game. If I was able to keep hidden right outside the saloon, I might have a chance to get word to him when the deranged gambler showed up to take his revenge on the best sheriff in the history of the great state of Kansas.

It was time to put this problem aside and refocus on

Abby and Tommy. They had been away from their parents for more than two weeks now. I felt awful for Mr. and Mrs. Walker. They had to be in sheer agony. I wanted to relieve their pain in the worst way, but I just wasn't sure how. Even though we had struck out at the Kimball ranch and the Hailey farm, I was still convinced that either of them, or both of them, had something to do with the abduction. I even found myself dismissing all other theories. I decided to concentrate on Fred and Mrs. Hailey, and only Fred and Mrs. Hailey. I wanted to return to both of their homes in the worst way and begin a second search—an even more thorough search. I'd look behind walls and under rafters. But I was a little nervous about returning to either location alone. And I doubted if the sheriff would agree to accompany me there. I knew he would feel that a second search at either place was a waste of time.

I continued down Main Street deep in thought. I eventually sat down on a patch of grass right outside the livery stable. I pulled the map from my pocket and studied it. Then I turned it over and decided to sketch out everything I could remember from our searches of the Kimball ranch and the Hailey farm. Unfortunately, I had nothing to write with. I got up and went into the livery stable. Jeremiah was feeding one of the horses.

"Jeremiah?"

"Hi, Pete."

"I wonder if I could ask you a favor."

"Sure, what is it?"

"Would you by any chance have a pencil or something I could write with?"

"Let me see. I was just using a pencil. Now where did I put it?" He looked on the counter by the front door. Not there. He checked all of his pockets. Not there either. He looked in a saddle bag hanging on a hook. Nothing. "Where the heck did I put that bugger?" He continued looking.

A moment later, I spotted it. It was wedged behind his ear. "Jeremiah?"

"Yeah?"

I pointed to his ear.

He felt for it and smiled. "Well, what do you know? I had it all along." He slipped it out and handed to me.

"Thanks," I said. "I won't be long."

"Take yer time."

I walked back outside to the same spot of grass. I began to draw what I would only call a rude blueprint of each house, room by room, floor by floor. I even sketched where the furniture was placed. Then I drew the barns. I included hay lofts and stalls. I plotted out the distance from the Walker farm to the Kimball house, and the Walker farm to the Hailey house. I sketched the field where Abby and Tommy were last seen before they disappeared. Then I tried to gauge how far they would have had to walk and at what speed to end up at either location. The more I drew, the more I realized they simply couldn't have walked the entire way to either spot. They had to have been on horseback or in a buckboard. Now the Mrs. Hailey theory was looking better. I continued drawing and sketching and jotting and plotting for the remainder of the afternoon. Before I knew it, the clock on the front of the stage office read six p.m. It was dinnertime. I walked back to the sheriff's office to retrieve my dinner companion.

When I got there, he was putting his boots on. Apparently, he had taken a short siesta.

"Pete, would you mind running over to Doc's and seeing if he's free for dinner?"

"Okay," I said. I ran into the street and headed for Doc's. With things now starting to heat up in Abilene, I was careful to avoid horses and buggies and wagons. When I got to Doc's, the door was ajar, so I walked in. The foyer was empty.

"Doc," I yelled out.

"I'll be with you in a minute," a voice said from behind a door halfway closed. I decided to take a seat in the waiting from. From there, I could hear a rather heated conversation going on in the next room. I leaned in closer to hear it.

"I can't give you something for a fever if you don't have a fever," Doc said.

"But I feel a fever coming on," a voice said.

I had heard that voice before. It was a woman's voice. Who the heck was it? And then I recognized it—Mrs. Hailey.

"Ma'am, your temperature is normal. You are perfectly healthy."

"Can't I have the medicine so I won't have to come all the way back here when the fever starts?"

"Rebecca, that's not how it works. I only give out medicine to sick people."

"Please, Doc. Don't make me beg. For years, I didn't believe in doctors. But I can't let it happen again. I need something for a fever. And I need it now."

Doc sighed loudly. "Here are three willow bark tablets. They should bring a fever down. Are you happy?"

"You're a difficult man to deal with, Dr. Conrad," she said. "I have a mind to take my business elsewhere in the future."

"Well, since I'm the only doctor in a fifty-mile radius, I don't think you'll have too many options."

"What do I owe you?" she said.

"That'll be fifteen cents."

"Ahh, just put it on my bill." Mrs. Hailey shot past me and was out the door in seconds.

Doc emerged a minute later. He looked at me and shook his head. "Can you believe that woman? She wants something for a fever, but she doesn't have a fever. She's losing her mind."

I smiled. "The sheriff wants to know if you're free for dinner."

"Sure, tell him I'll meet him over there."

I got up to leave and suddenly had a revelation. My mouth went dry. My legs were rubbery.

"Oh my god!" I'll see you, Doc.

I sprinted to the livery stable.

"Jeremiah, can you saddle up Shuffle. I need him right away."

Jeremiah stuck his head out of the stable door. "It's gonna be dark pretty soon, Pete. Are you sure about this?"

"Yes, please."

"Okay, then, he'll be ready in a few minutes."

"Thanks." I ran back to the sheriff's office. When I got there, I threw the door open.

"Sheriff, we have to go out to Mrs. Hailey's place. Hurry. I know for a fact the kids are there."

"What are you talking about?"

"I was just over at Doc's and Mrs. Hailey was in there talking to him. She was asking for something for a fever, but she didn't have a fever. She was arguing with Doc. He didn't want to give her medicine since she appeared perfectly healthy. We have to get over there. Let's go."

"Whoa, slow down. I don't understand."

"Don't you see. The medicine's not for her. It's gotta be for someone else. And that someone else has gotta be either Abby or Tommy. She *does* have them. C'mon."

"Maybe she has relatives visiting," he said.

"Then where were they when we searched her place? It's for one of the kids. I know it."

"Pete, I just can't see us dropping everything and rushing over there. We searched that place. The kids weren't—" He stopped. A smile began to form on his face. "Wait a minute. Wait just a minute. I see what's happening here. You're pretty clever, young man," the sheriff said. "You almost had me going for there for a minute."

"What are you talking about?"

"*What are you talking about*? As if you didn't know. I see right through you, Pete Moss. You know I plan to play poker tonight. And you're trying to convince me not to play. So, you come up with this whopper of a story to get me to go out to Mrs. Hailey's and miss the game."

"What?! No, that's not it at all. Mrs. Hailey really was at Doc's. And she wanted medicine, but she wasn't sick. I'm not trying to trick you. I promise. You can ask him."

He rubbed the top of my head. "You're a little too clever for your own good." He grabbed his hat from the hook and opened the door. "It's dinnertime. C'mon."

I just stood there. I didn't know what to do. Do I go to Mrs. Hailey's and try to find those kids? Or do I stick around here and try to prevent the death of Sheriff Amos *Lone Wolf* Malone? I rubbed my forehead. Which one was more important? If I went all the way to the Hailey farm and couldn't find the kids, I would have failed on both ends. I pressed my temples with both hands. Think, Pete, think. A minute later, I had the answer. It might work. It just might work.

CHAPTER 22

I SAT AT THE SHERIFF'S DESK AND WROTE THE FOLLOWING
note:

> *When you're dealt a hand of two aces and*
> *two eights, look over your shoulder.*

    I knew from what I had previously read about Amos
Malone that on the fateful night, he was seated with his
back to the door because none of the other gamblers
would agree to switch places with him. I also knew that
Moses Tanahill would stop in tonight for his revenge on
the man who had taken the bulk of his money the night
before. I knew the sheriff would be holding a hand of aces
and eights when the actual event took place. I only hoped
he would turn to see Tanahill in time.

    I folded up the note and left it on top of the safe. Since
the sheriff would come back to the office after dinner to
pick up his gambling money, I knew he would have to go
into the safe. I put "Sheriff Malone - IMPORTANT" on the

outside of the note. He would have to see it. Since I had never written anything to him in cursive before, he wouldn't recognize my handwriting. That was critical. Knowing how stubborn he was about not being told anything about the future, I knew if he thought I had written it, he might not read the note. I was fairly certain he would open it up and read it before he realized I was the one who had actually tipped him off about what was to occur tonight. I could guarantee he wouldn't be happy about it, but that was just too bad. I had a chance to save the man's life, and I wasn't about to whiff on that.

I grabbed my hat and headed over to the livery stable. Shuffle was all ready to go. I jumped on and took off. I headed directly toward Mrs. Hailey's house. The sun was setting. It would be dark soon. I wasn't a huge fan of traveling at night since I wasn't completely certain of my surroundings, but I was fairly sure of where I was going. I began to think about what I would say to Mrs. Hailey when I got there. I needed to convince her that a second search was required. She likely wouldn't be too happy about it, but that was just too bad. I was a deputy sheriff, and I had the authority to do this. The problem was that I would need a new approach to this search. I couldn't just look in closets and under beds. I needed to check behind walls and cupboards. But how would I know which walls to inspect? I couldn't just tear the place apart. What I needed was x-ray vision. I needed to see behind things. How would I know if the kids were being held in a secret compartment if I couldn't see it? I thought long and hard. Nothing was popping into my head. Then, out of nowhere, I had it. I pulled back on the reins and brought Shuffle to a stop.

"Of course," I said out loud. "Killer!"

I knew exactly what I had to do. I needed to change course and head to the Walker house. I would need to ask Mr. and Mrs. Walker if I could borrow Killer for a little while. Since he was Abby's dog, he would instantly know her scent. All I would have to do is let him loose in the Hailey house, and he would point to the exact location of the kids' whereabouts. It was a brilliant idea. I didn't know why I hadn't thought of it before. With Killer's assistance, I was sure I would find the kids. But if for some reason I didn't, I would take him with me to the Kimball ranch and let him do the same thing there. Between the two locations, I was certain I'd have success.

I rode hard to the Walker house. By the time I had gotten there, the sun had set. It was getting darker by the minute. I jumped off Shuffle, led him to a water trough right outside the house, and tied him up. He could get refreshed while I was talking to Abby's parents. I walked up and knocked on the front door. A moment later, Mr. Walker appeared.

"Pete, is that you?"

"Yes, sir."

"Come on in."

I entered the house and looked around. I didn't see Abby's mom.

"So, what can we do for you?" he said.

"I was wondering if I could borrow Killer for a little while."

"Killer?"

"Yeah, I need to search a location we're investigating, and I thought he might be able to pick up Abby's scent if she's close by."

"Well, of course, anything to help. C'mon, he's in the barn."

"Who is it?" a voice came from another room. Mrs. Walker appeared in the doorway. She looked even worse than she had since the last time I saw her.

"Hello, Pete," she said weakly.

"Pete needs to borrow Killer for a little while," Mr. Walker said.

"What in heavens for?" she said.

"They're investigating someplace where they think Abby and Tommy might be. He wants to see if Killer might be able to point him in Abby's direction."

"Oh, well, that's wonderful," she said.

"We're headed to the barn right now," Abby's dad said.

"Don't let me keep you," she said. "We appreciate everything you and Sheriff Malone are doing for us."

"No need, ma'am. That's our job."

"Come on, Pete," Mr. Walker said.

I waved to Abby's mom as I headed out into the farmyard. I followed Mr. Walker to the barn. As soon as he opened the door, Killer came running out. He started barking rather aggressively at first, but then when he recognized me and Mr. Walker, he quieted down and began wagging his tail.

"I've got some rope around here somewhere," Mr. Walker said. He looked for a minute before finding it. He crouched down and tied one end to Killer's collar. He handed the other end to me. He put his hand on my shoulder.

"I pray this will be the answer we're looking for. Please let us know immediately if you find anything."

"I definitely will," I said. I hopped up on Shuffle and tied the end of the rope to the saddle horn. I hoped Killer could keep up with us. I waved goodbye and was off. It took me a second or two to get my bearings in the dark but before long I was pretty sure I knew the way to the Hailey house. My worries about Killer keeping up with Shuffle were soon gone. He was out in front and leading us the entire way. It was almost as if he knew exactly where we were headed. It was relatively easy to keep an eye on the little guy since he was all white. It was like having a light leading our way. We rode for a good twenty minutes before coming up on the Hailey farm. I approached cautiously. I hopped down and walked with Shuffle the last hundred yards. When I had made it onto her property, I didn't see any lights on in the house. Good, I thought. She must not be home. Even though I wasn't completely comfortable entering someone else's house when they weren't there, I definitely preferred conducting this search with her gone.

I tied Shuffle to a hitching post right outside the house. I untied the rope from the saddle horn and was about to lead Killer up to the front door, but he did it for me. He was pulling hard on the rope. It was as if he knew something I didn't. I knocked on the door and waited. A few seconds later, I knocked again. When I was fairly certain no one was home, I turned the doorknob. It was locked. I went around to the side, and then to the back of the house where I found a window partially open. I slid it open the rest of the way and lifted Killer up into the house. I climbed in after him. I immediately spotted a kerosene lantern on the table. I fumbled around for a while until I found some matches. I assumed Mrs. Hailey would walk in that door any minute so I needed to be quick.

"Killer," I said. "Lead the way, buddy."

Killer seemed interested in one thing and one thing

only—a bearskin rug in the middle of the floor. He began sniffing it and barking at it.

"That thing's dead, Killer. Don't worry about it. Come on, we have to check the rest of the house." It took me a while to get him to leave that spot. I started walking him all the way around the house. He would sniff a little but then look back in the direction of that rug. Once more we searched the entire house but found nothing.

"C'mon, let's hit the barn."

I tried to lead Killer out of the house, but he refused to budge. He grabbed hold of the rug with his teeth. As I pulled him out the front door, he still had the rug in his mouth. I shook my head. What was wrong with this dog anyway? I managed to get the rug from him and re-entered the house to put it back in place. As I was standing there, I couldn't believe what I was seeing. There was a door in the floor—a trapdoor. It had been hidden by the rug. It was the same kind of trapdoor that was in the sheriff's office. Killer was now clawing at the door. There was a metal bolt keeping it closed. I ran to the front door and looked out. I needed to see if Mrs. Hailey was in sight. So far, so good. I ran back and slid the bolt, unlocking the door. I opened it and looked in. I couldn't see a thing. It was pitch black inside. I wasn't sure what I would find down there. There might be rats or mice or bats or other vermin. I wasn't interested in meeting up with any of them. I could see a ladder that led down to somewhere. I picked up the lantern and held it over the crawl space. I couldn't see much this way. I would have to go down there myself to check it out. I was suddenly wishing the sheriff had been with me.

I began to breathe rapidly. I could feel my heart racing. I wasn't sure I wanted to do this. But since Killer was so intent on getting down into that hole, I knew I had to. I slowly climbed down the ladder with one hand, and held the lantern with the other. When I got down to the dirt floor, I looked up. Killer's head was hanging over the hole. He wanted to get down there in the worst way. I set the lantern on the floor and climbed back up. I grabbed hold of Killer with one arm wrapped around his stomach and slowly descended into the hole. He jumped from my arms when I hit the last rung. He immediately made a beeline for the far corner of the crawlspace. I picked up the lantern and followed him over. When I got there, I found a door leading into another room. Killer was clawing at the door. When I opened it and held up the lantern, my jaw dropped.

"Oh, my god! Oh, my god!" I yelled. I was staring at Abby and Tommy. They were alive. Mrs. Hailey had bound and gagged both of them. She had tied up their arms and legs. I ran over to Abby and pulled the gag off her mouth. Killer ran up to her and began licking her face.

"Oh, Pete, Pete," she said. "I can't believe you found us. Thank God."

"Are you okay?" I asked. I felt her forehead. She was warm.

"I don't feel well, but that's okay. I'm just so happy to see you."

I untied her arms, then her legs. She tried to stand but her legs were wobbly. She took a step and collapsed into my arms.

"It's okay. I've got you." I set her down and began to untie Tommy. He was crying. "You're safe now. There's nothing to be worried about."

"Abby's sick," he said. "You have to help her."

"I plan on doing just that." I lifted Tommy off the floor and carried him over to the ladder. "Wait right here for me." I went back for Abby. I helped her up. She had very little strength. She was leaning on me as we walked to the ladder. I set her down gently. "Okay, Tommy, jump onto my back. We're headed out of this place."

Suddenly I heard a noise from above. I motioned for the kids to stay quiet. Seconds later, Mrs. Hailey stuck her head into the hole. She was staring right at me. And she was smiling, but in a weird sort of way.

"It's so nice to see you again, Pete. I see you've come for our little family reunion. I couldn't be happier. Now don't get any thoughts about leaving. This is your new home. I hope you'll be happy here."

"You can't get away with this," I said. "The sheriff's on his way over. He'll be here any minute now. And he'll find us."

"I don't think so," she said. A moment later, she dropped a small vial of pills through the trapdoor opening. "Make sure Abby takes these. It'll help with her fever." She slammed the door shut.

I could hear her slide the metal bolt in place. I looked over at Abby. Her head dropped.

"Oh, no. Oh, no," she said. "Well, I'm sure as heck not taking those pills. Who knows what they are."

"I wanna go home," Tommy said through tears.

"Don't worry. We're gonna get out of here. It's just a matter of time."

"So, is the sheriff really coming over here?" Abby asked.

I looked down and shook my head. "No, I just told her that. He's back in town playing poker." I thought about the sheriff. I wondered if he had read my note. I hoped so. I also wondered if Moses Tanahill had made his appearance at the saloon yet. I could only pray that when the sheriff was dealt what had become known as the *Dead Man's Hand*, a pair of aces and a pair of eights, that he had glanced over his shoulder in time to avoid Tanahill's assault. But I couldn't think about that now. I had bigger problems on my hands.

CHAPTER 23

We all sat quietly for several minutes without uttering a word. The thought of freedom being snatched away so quickly had to have been a devastating blow to Abby and Tommy. I couldn't imagine how they were able to survive down here for the better part of two weeks. These conditions were inhumane. I wasn't sure if Mrs. Hailey was sick or evil, or maybe a little of both. Whatever it was, she had to be stopped. And the responsibility to do so fell squarely on my shoulders. I had to figure out a way out of here. I couldn't wait for the sheriff to come looking for us. Of course, first he would have to survive the attack from a deranged gambler. And even if he were able to do so, it was doubtful he'd be able to locate this crawlspace without the help of Killer. We had both missed it the first time out here.

I wasn't sure how much longer we would have light. The kerosene in the lantern wouldn't last forever. I got up and began checking all of the walls. I wanted to see if there was any other way out of here.

"It's no use," Abby said. "We've looked for another escape route a million times."

"The only way out is straight up," Tommy said, pointing at the trap door.

"That's what I was afraid of," I said. I wondered how long it would be before someone came looking for us. I never bothered to tell the Walkers where I was taking Killer. They'd have no reason to come out here. But the sheriff would know. I had told him I suspected Mrs. Hailey and I wanted to come out here to look again. Even if he did eventually come out here, it was doubtful he could ever find this crawlspace. I came to the conclusion that I couldn't wait to be saved. I would have to figure a way out myself.

I climbed the ladder and began pounding on the trap door. I wondered if I had the strength to bend or break the bolt. But I could quickly tell it wasn't budging. Trying to break out was not an option. I supposed we could wait until someone showed up and then start screaming at the top of our lungs and hope we were heard. Maybe we could even get Killer to bark loudly as well. Someone might hear us. The problem was that we wouldn't know when someone else was in the house, or if someone would ever show up. I was feeling like such a failure.

"So, how did you guys survive all this time down here?"

"Mrs. Hailey would feed us occasionally," Abby said.

"Yeah, those were the only times she ever untied our hands," Tommy said.

"What about light?" I said. "Could you see anything down here?"

"The only times there was any light was when she

opened the door," Abby said. "But when you've been locked up in the dark for so long in the same place, you get a pretty good idea where things are at after a while. It's really nice to have that lantern though."

"But for how long?" I said. "The kerosene will eventually run out."

"Is it day or night?" Abby asked. "I can never tell."

"It's night," I said.

"We would never know when it was time to stay awake or go to sleep," she said. "I suppose we slept a lot more than we needed to, but there was nothing else to do."

"So, would you guys talk to her? What would she say?"

"I did most of the talking for us," Abby said. "Tommy cried a lot."

"I did not," he said.

"Would she tell you why she brought you here?"

"She would tell us this crazy story that our parents didn't want us around anymore, and they asked her to take care of us," Abby said. "We knew it wasn't true. And when I'd ask if we could go over to our house and find out for ourselves, she got really angry and told us we would never be able to go home again—ever." Abby paused. "Oh, and one more thing. Occasionally she would call me Heather."

"Heather?" I said. "Where have I heard that name before? Wait a minute. That was the name of her daughter —the one who died."

"Oh, now that makes sense," Abby said. "I never knew her name."

"Where did you guys sleep? Are there any beds or mattresses down here?"

Tommy pointed to the room I had found them in. "We

have some blankets in there, but the floor is really hard. And it's cold."

The entire time Killer sat at Abby's feet. He had been reunited with his best friend and he wasn't budging.

I sat down on the dirt floor and eventually rolled over on my side. I was getting tired. When I did that, I felt something poking me in the thigh. I reached into my pocket and pulled out the magnet I'd been carrying around since I had gotten here. I set it down next to me.

"What's that?" Tommy asked.

"Oh, it's called a magnet."

"Can I hold it?" he said.

I handed it to him.

"It's heavy. What's it for."

"Well, at school, I used it to—" Whoops, I almost slipped. I couldn't tell them where I came from or how I got here. "You put it next to a piece of metal, and it'll stick to it."

"I wish I could see how it worked," Tommy said.

I looked around to see if I could find anything that it might stick to. There was no metal in sight.

"Well, when we get out of here, I'll show you how it works." I slid the magnet back into my pocket.

"*If* we get out of here," Abby said.

"Don't say that. I'm gonna get you guys outta here. I promise."

Abby smiled. "I hope you're right."

I let out a long, loud yawn. "I must be getting tired."

"Why don't you lie down for a while," Abby said. "Then we'll try to figure out how to get out of here. Maybe you'll be able to think more clearly when you're rested."

I nodded and yawned again.

"I'll get you a blanket," she said.

"No, I'm fine. You guys use them."

"We have plenty," she said.

A moment later, Abby returned with an old, holey, smelly blanket. I would have preferred not using it, but since she had gone to the trouble of getting it for me, I thought it best to just suck it up and use it.

"Thanks. This is great." I spread out the blanket and lay down on it. Tommy was right. The ground was cold and hard. Hopefully I wouldn't be here for more than a few hours. I glanced at the others. They were looking tired as well.

"Even though we're still locked up," Tommy said. "I feel better with you here, Pete."

"I'm glad. And don't worry, I'll think of something."

I lay back on the blanket and closed my eyes. It would be really easy to fall asleep right now, but I really should be trying to think of a way to get us out of here. These two were counting on me. I needed to brainstorm for a while. I hoped...I prayed...I could think of some way to escape. Before long, I had fallen asleep. When I woke up, I had no idea how long I had been out. Both Abby and Tommy were asleep. The kerosene lantern was flickering. The light would soon be out. I needed to come up with a plan while we could still see what we were doing. I rolled over and felt the magnet sticking me again. I took it out of my pocket and was about to throw it across the room when I suddenly stopped. Wait a minute. Wait just a minute. I know exactly where to find some metal. And it might just be our way out. I grabbed for the magnet and glanced up at the trapdoor. I wondered if I could slide the magnet across the door and move the metal bolt just enough to open it.

I climbed the ladder with magnet in hand. I tried to recall the exact position of the metal bolt, and which direction I would have to move it to slide it open. I would have to do this as quietly as possible to avoid having Mrs. Hailey hear it. I held the magnet against the inside of the trapdoor and tried to move it ever so slowly. Then I would try to push up to see if I had gotten it. The first attempt was unsuccessful. As was the second, third, fourth, and eventually, the tenth.

I wondered if the door was too thick. The magnet might not be able to move it. I shook my head. Darn it! I was so sure this would work. I decided to keep trying. It was our only hope. I stayed at it for the next five minutes, which soon turned into fifteen minutes, and then thirty minutes. I was about to give up when I thought to myself. I wondered if I was using the wrong end of the magnet. Could that be possible? I flipped it over to the other side and began the same process. I'd slide it to one side, then lean my shoulder into the door to see if it budged. Repeated attempts proved futile. Then, when I was ready to throw in the towel, I positioned the magnet in a slightly different spot and slid it over. Wait a minute. Did I just hear something? I pushed up on the door...and it moved. It actually moved. I raised it slowly so it wouldn't slam when it hit the floor.

"Yessssss!" I said. Apparently, I had spoken a little too loudly.

Abby had awakened. She got up and ran over. "Pete, is that door open? Is it really open? How'd you do it?"

"I'll explain that later. Can you climb up here on your own or do you need help?"

"I think I can do it, but let's send Tommy up first."

Abby hurried over and tugged Tommy on the arm. "Tommy, wake up. It's time to go."

He sat up and rubbed his eyes.

She led him over to the ladder. "Look up there," she said, pointing at me still standing on the top rung. "Can you climb up that ladder?"

"I sure can."

I lowered myself to the ground.

Tommy literally flew up the ladder and quietly climbed out. Abby followed. Then me. We were all standing next to the trapdoor when Killer let loose. He apparently thought we were going to leave him. He started barking.

"No, Killer!" Abby said. "Not now!"

"I'll get him," I said. I climbed down, wrapped my arm around him, and headed back up. When I was near the top, I handed him to Abby. Then I stepped onto the floor and stopped in my tracks. Standing in front of us, blocking the door, holding a rifle, was Mrs. Hailey.

"This had to be your doing, Pete. I can smell it. But no matter," she said. "Now I want you to turn around and go back down that ladder real nice like."

Tommy started to cry.

"Quit your blubbering," she shouted.

Abby set Killer on the floor and put her arm around her brother.

"I have news for you, ma'am," I said. "We're not going back to your dungeon. We're walking out the front door. And you can't stop us."

Killer started barking and began to growl.

"Shut that dog up!" Mrs. Hailey snapped. "Or I'll finish him off right here."

"No," Abby said. She crouched down and put her arms around him.

"I'm not gonna tell you again. Get back down there."

"We're not going," I said. I wasn't sure why I was talking so tough. I had no reason to. There was no way she was going to let us walk out that door.

"It appears we have a standoff, young man." She held up the rifle. "But guess who's gonna win."

"You should know that the sheriff is on his way as we speak. He'll be here any minute."

"Nice try," she said. "Now I'm not gonna tell you again. Move!"

I looked down at Killer. And then I remembered something—the magic word.

"Killer," I yelled as I pointed at Mrs. Hailey. "Nonoma! Nonoma, Killer!" And with that command, Killer broke free from Abby's grasp and was on Mrs. Hailey before she knew what hit her. He was growling and scratching and biting. She dropped the rifle to the ground. I ran over and grabbed it as I pulled our trusty attack dog off of her. I untied the rope that was still tied to Killer's collar.

I handed the rifle to Abby. "Hold this while I tie her up." I plopped Mrs. Hailey in a chair and proceeded to tie her hands and feet.

"I didn't kidnap these children. That delinquent, Fred Kimball, was behind all of it."

Fred Kimball. I had a feeling that name would pop up. We'd have to take care of him in due time.

For good measure, I decided to tie the chair to a post in the room. And since she wouldn't stop screaming at us, I found a rag in a drawer and gagged her.

"That ought to keep you quiet for a while."

She continued to spew gibberish at us.

"Come on," I said. "She's got a buckboard in the barn. We'll use that." I ran out across the farmyard and into the barn. I quickly harnessed a horse to the buckboard. I tied Shuffle to the back. "Let's go," I yelled as I pulled out of the barn. Abby and Tommy climbed on board and we were off. We had done it. We had managed a successful escape. Abby and Tommy were headed home.

CHAPTER 24

TWENTY MINUTES LATER, WE WERE PULLING UP IN FRONT OF the Walker house. I had no idea what time it was, but I knew it was the middle of the night. The house was completely dark. I didn't think Mr. and Mrs. Walker would mind being awakened this early. I jumped down off the buckboard and helped Tommy down, and then Abby. When I set her on the ground, she looked at me and smiled. Then she threw her arms around me and gave me the tightest hug I had ever received from a girl before. It was amazing.

"I don't know how I'll ever be able to thank you. You saved our lives."

"You're very welcome. I'm just so happy we found you guys. Seeing you safely back home is all the thanks I need."

We walked up to the front door. Tommy opened it and walked in.

"Is anybody home?" he yelled out.

A moment later, Mr. Walker appeared, still in his long johns. He was holding a lantern.

"Oh, my god! Oh, my god! Martha, come here quickly."
He grabbed Tommy and picked him up. He squeezed him
and spun him around. "My boy, my boy." Then he reached
out for Abby and pulled her in tightly. "My princess,
you're back home."

Mrs. Walker squealed when she saw the kids. "Oh,
thank you, Lord, thank you!" She reached out and held
one child in each arm. She refused to let go, and who
could blame her. This had to be the best day of her life.
And I, for one, was happy to be part of it.

Killer was standing at our feet, panting. Mr. Walker
bent down to pet him.

"Pete, how did you find them?"

"It really wasn't me. It was all Killer. He led me right to
them."

"Don't be so modest, Pete," Abby said. "You knew just
where to look."

We sat down for a few minutes and I shared a
condensed version with the Walkers of what had taken
place in the last eight hours. They had a hard time
believing Mrs. Hailey had abducted both children and
held them hostage in her crawlspace for the past two
weeks. When I told them about Killer's role in all of this,
they were equally amazed. He had not only located the
exact spot they were being held, he also disarmed Mrs.
Hailey, and made this homecoming possible. Mrs. Walker
never let go of her kids the entire time I spoke.

"We'll never be able to thank you enough," Mrs.
Walker said.

"No thanks necessary. It was all part of the job." I
smiled. "I'm going to head into town now and bring back
Doc. Abby felt a little warm to me a little while ago. I
think he should take a look at her."

Mrs. Walker immediately felt her daughter's forehead. "She is warm, Hiram."

"And what do you suppose will happen to that woman, Pete?" Mr. Walker asked.

"I plan to bring the sheriff out to her house to make the arrest. Right now, we have her tied up. Then I guess she'll be tossed in jail until the trial."

"She's a horrible woman," Mr. Walker said. "I hope she gets everything that's coming to her."

"Hiram, she's sick," his wife said. "She must be. Who else would steal someone else's children?"

"Well, she looked pretty healthy to me when she was holding that rifle on us," I said.

"I think she needs help," Mrs. Walker said.

"I guess that'll be up to the courts," I said. "Well, I'm headed out. I just wanted to make sure Abby and Tommy got home safely." I tipped my hat and headed for the door. Before I reached it, someone grabbed my arm. When I turned, I saw it was Abby.

"Thanks again," she said. "I'll never forget you." She hugged me and kissed me on the cheek.

Right at that moment, I was feeling ten feet tall. I literally floated out to the barnyard and hopped up onto Shuffle. I headed for town. This was going to be one sweet ride. The sun was just coming up. I was thinking how little sleep I had gotten, but for some reason I wasn't tired. I must have been on some sort of adrenaline rush. And then my thoughts turned to Sheriff Malone. I wondered what I would find when I got to town. Had he seen my note? Had he read it? Had he looked over his shoulder when he drew a hand of aces and eights? Good or bad, I would know these answers very soon.

When I arrived in Abilene, things appeared pretty

normal. If the town had lost its sheriff the night before, there was nothing that indicated as much. I headed in the direction of Doc Conrad's office. On the way, I passed Jeremiah as he was opening up the livery stable. He waved. As did Mr. Crowley who was sweeping in front of the General Store. As I made my way to Doc's, I heard some banging coming from a storefront that read *Mortician*. I had seen the word before. I was fairly sure it was someone who buried the dead. When I got closer, I peeked through the window. I saw a man hammering a nail into what appeared to be a coffin. A coffin?! No, it couldn't be! It just couldn't! I poked my head in. I had to know.

"Excuse me," I said to the man.

He set down his hammer. "Yes, can I help you, young man?"

"Um...could I ask who that coffin is for?"

"It's for the sheriff," he said.

My heart sank. I couldn't believe it. I started to feel nauseous. Hadn't the sheriff seen my note? Did he recognize my handwriting and ignore it? Why did this have to happen? I started feeling guilty—really really guilty. My decision to look for the Walker kids had seemed like the number one priority. Apparently, I should have saved the sheriff's life first, and then continued to search for the kids. If I had found them a few hours later, it wouldn't have made much difference. I had really screwed this up. I had had a month to prepare for this, and I had completely messed up. I headed to Doc's office with a heavy heart. It was pretty early, but I had to find out exactly what had happened at that poker game. I needed to know details of how and why my plan had failed.

When I arrived at Doc's, I immediately noticed the sheriff's horse parked out front. I wondered what would happen to him. I didn't know if the sheriff had a will or not. I walked up the stairs and knocked on the door. It took Doc a minute or two to answer it.

"Pete, where have you been? We've been worried about you?"

"I've been kind of busy the last few hours to tell you the truth."

"Doing what?" Doc asked.

I wasn't interested in making small talk with Doc. I wanted to know what had happened to the sheriff.

"Doc, um...how did things go down at that poker game last night?"

"Poker game? How should I know? I wasn't there."

"But you had to know about the sheriff. Someone had to have told you."

"What about the sheriff?"

Right at that moment, I heard a noise coming from another room. When I turned to see what it was, my jaw dropped. Standing in the doorway was Amos Lone Wolf Malone in all his glory. His arm was in a sling.

"Sh...sh...sheriff, you're not dead! I just passed by the mortician and he said he was making a coffin for you. I don't understand."

"Yeah, late last night, I asked him to make a coffin for me."

I threw my head back and exhaled loudly. "I thought the coffin was for *you*. You know, for you to lie in it."

He chuckled.

I ran over and threw my arms around him. "I am soooo glad to see you!"

"Well, it's nice to see you too, Deputy."

"I guess this means you got my note?"

He grinned. "I did. Thank you." He put his arm

around me. "I know what I told you about warning me about the future and all...but I'm really glad you did. I had a chance to think about things in that split second, and I decided I wanted to live. You saved my life."

"What happened to your arm?"

"Well, as you can guess, I kept waiting to be dealt the aces and eights hand. When I picked up my cards about eleven-thirty, I was staring directly at them. I immediately spun around and found Moses Tanahill standing there with his gun drawn. We both fired. He clipped me. My aim was a little better. I dropped him. He fell to the floor. The coffin is for him." He rubbed his shoulder. "Doc removed the bullet and patched me up a few hours ago."

I was happy and relieved and ecstatic and every other emotion you can imagine.

"Here's something you'll find interesting. Last night after all of the commotion had died down, I went back to the saloon to say good night to a few folks, and guess who I found standing at the bar?"

"Who?"

"Our friendly buffalo hunters."

"Really?"

"Yep. I confronted them about the Cheyenne boy. They weren't expecting it. Just to be safe, I decided to question them separately. As you might guess, they came up with two completely different stories. They eventually blamed the other one for beating up the boy. It didn't take me long to throw their sorry butts in the slammer. They'll have their day in court soon. I might invite Chief White Deer to the festivities to see for himself how we handle cutthroats." He smiled. "So, tell me. Where have you been? I was about to go out and look for you."

"It's kind of a long story."

The sheriff sat down. "I got nothing but time."

So, for the next ten minutes, I told him the entire story —about heading out to Mrs. Hailey's; abruptly changing course when I thought about using Killer to help; going to the Walker's to pick up their three-legged attack dog; traveling back to Mrs. Hailey's; entering her house and letting Killer start the search; noticing his interest with the bearskin rug; finding out what was actually underneath it; making my descent into the crawlspace; my discovery of Abby and Tommy in a small room under the house; the condition I found them in; being surprised by Mrs. Hailey and finding ourselves locked down there again; my brainstorm when I thought about the magnet; opening the door; escaping to only find Mrs. Hailey standing there holding a rifle; uttering the magic word that sent Killer into attack mode; tying her up in her house; her admission of Fred Kimball as her accomplice; and returning the kids to their parents.

"Pete, you're a hero!" Doc exclaimed. "You're a genuine hero!"

"I just did what the sheriff taught me to do. That was all. And, Doc, I actually came to here to bring you back to the Walker's. Abby has a fever."

"Oh dear, let me pack up my bag right away. Pete, how did the children seem after their ordeal?"

"Pretty good, if you ask me."

"I'll want to check both of them out."

"Hey, partner," the sheriff said. "We'd better go pick up our prisoners. What do you say?"

"Sounds good."

We accompanied Doc out to the Walker's to see how the kids were doing and to get their official statements regarding the abduction. I was perfectly fine with that. It gave me one more chance to see Abby. Then we swung over to Mrs. Hailey's. We found her on the floor. In her attempts to free herself, all she had managed to do was knock over the chair. The sheriff questioned her right there. She was only too happy to give up Fred Kimball. Apparently, she knew it would be difficult to convince the kids to go with her to her house, so she paid Fred to find the kids in the field and tell them their dad had been injured in a farming accident. They began to follow him back to their home until he changed course and headed for Mrs. Hailey's. When the Walker kids refused to go there, he strong-armed them, dragging them to the Hailey farm. In an emotional display, Mrs. Hailey began to cry when she spoke about losing her own daughter. She told the sheriff how much she wanted children again. She said she was sorry for what she had done. But I wasn't sure if she was sorry about kidnapping the children, or sorry about getting caught.

Then it was on to the Kimball ranch. That encounter was a bit dicey. When we got there, Fred's parents were home. His dad was not inclined to let the sheriff haul his only son off to jail. But with Mrs. Hailey there to tell her side of the story, it didn't take long for Fred to crack. He kept blaming the old woman for putting him up to it. We eventually cuffed Fred and took him back to town. He only spent one night in jail. Since his dad had deep pockets, he was bailed out relatively quickly. Mrs. Hailey and the buffalo hunters, however, were refused bail, and spent many a night in the Abilene jail.

Word spread fast around town about my role in finding the missing children. Everyone who saw me on the streets would stop to shake my hand. After a while, people started calling me *"The Abilene Kid."* It felt really good, but it was a little embarrassing. Whenever they'd congratulate me, I would just give credit to Killer. Most people dismissed the efforts of a three-legged dog. But Abby, Tommy, and I knew better. We never stopped singing Killer's praises.

In the days following our dramatic escape, I had visited the Walker farm every few days to spend time with Abby. We would go for long walks, feed the chickens, do chores together, or just sit on the front porch swing. I was really enjoying the time we spent together. But after a while, I could sense an unhappiness in her. She said it had nothing to do with me. Rather, it was due to the trauma she experienced while locked in Mrs. Hailey's dungeon. Her parents noticed the same thing. They decided she needed a change of scenery. The recent memories in Abilene were just too painful. So, Mrs. Walker and Abby went to visit her cousin in Kansas City. They planned to spend the rest of the summer there.

Needless to say, I was pretty bummed out. Abby was one of the reasons I enjoyed living in Abilene in 1888. Without her around, things weren't the same. As the days went on, nothing quite as exciting as returning an injured Cheyenne boy to his reservation or tracking down a pair of missing kids seemed to occur. And to be quite honest, I was starting to get really homesick. Don't get me wrong. I loved working alongside Sheriff Malone but I was kind of feeling that my work here was done. The sheriff was alive and would be around to keep the peace in Abilene for years to come. And I kind of missed the conveniences of home—especially air conditioning, the internet, and, of course, indoor plumbing.

One night when the sheriff and I were about to hit the

sack, I mentioned my desire to return home. It caught him off-guard.

"Really, Pete? Are you serious?"

"Kind of."

"Well, I don't want to keep you anywhere you don't want to be."

"It's not that, Sheriff. I love it here working with you, but I kind of miss my best friend, Will, and my folks, and...do you understand?"

"I do. I'm disappointed, but I understand. So, when were you thinking about leaving?"

I stared at the floor. "Now?" I said.

"I'm going to really miss you, Pete," he said.

"Sheriff, this was the greatest experience of my life. I'll never forget you. You're the best."

"You're sure about this now?"

"I think so."

"So, what am I gonna tell everyone when they notice the *Abilene Kid* is gone?"

"Hopefully, you'll think of something."

"Don't worry. I can handle that. Now remember, you're always welcome here anytime you like. The door is always open."

"Thanks, I might just take you up on that sometime."

The sheriff walked over to me. "Well, I guess this is it." He extended his hand, then threw his arms around me. He kissed the top of my head. "You're like the son I never had."

"If you had gotten married and started a family, you wouldn't need me, you know. And doesn't that brush with death make you think about Marian, and what your life might have been like if you two had gotten together?"

"I've actually thought about her a lot lately. I've considered asking her to dinner one of these nights."

"Fantastic!"

"Then there's nothing more for me to do here. Everything is working out beautifully."

He smiled. He reached down and pulled open the same trapdoor in the floor I had come through weeks ago.

"So, how does this work?"

"Just climb down that ladder and start walking through the tunnel. After about fifty yards, you'll see a door. When you open it, you'll be back in the library basement, and no time will have passed. It'll be as if you were never here."

"Don't say it like that," I said. "I'll never forget this place."

"And we'll never forget you. Good luck, son."

"Thanks." I smiled and did my best to hold back the tears. I dropped my head and climbed down the ladder. When I reached the bottom, I looked up. The sheriff waved and winked. Then he closed the door behind me. I began my trek through the long tunnel. A minute or so later, I could see a light coming from under the door. When I opened it, I stepped out into the library basement. I couldn't believe it. I was back in the present. And the first edition book I had been reading when all this happened was still lying on the table. I looked at the cover—*The Man Who Tamed the Wild West. The Unauthorized Biography of Amos "Lone Wolf" Malone.*

I opened the book and began paging through it. Then I stopped abruptly. I wonder if it's possible. Could it be? I had to find out. Would the changes that had taken place in the life of Sheriff Malone while I was there be reflected in this book? I had to know. I went to the index and searched for "marriage." It took me to page 114. And right there in bold print—*Amos Malone marries Marian Couture on December 12, 1888.* That was fantastic news. I couldn't believe it. Then I needed to check one more thing before I resumed my old life. I went to the index and looked for "death." I flipped to page 234 and began to read.

"Oh, no! Not again! It can't be! They were just newlyweds. Marian can't be a widow this soon." I had to do something. I had to stop this. I turned and stared at the door that read STAFF – NO ADMITTANCE. Could I get back to Abilene that way or would it actually be a library staff door now? I walked over and turned the knob. The door opened. I was staring at a long dark tunnel. It was time to rewrite history a second time. "I'm coming, Sheriff. I'm coming!"

A LOOK AT BOOK TWO:

THE ABILENE KID: BOOT HILL CURSE (THE ABILENE KID 2)

AN EPIC YA WESTERN TIME-TRAVEL ADVENTURE CONTINUES...

After saving Sheriff Amos Malone from a deadly poker game, twelve-year-old Pete Moss—formerly Dominick Dalesandro—thought his time-traveling days were over. But when he discovers that the sheriff had found himself in more trouble, Pete knows he has no choice but to return to 1888 Abilene, Kansas and rewrite history once again.

This time, Pete faces two deadly mysteries—clearing a buried man's name and uncovering a powerful townsperson's dark secret. As he pieces the truth together, a brutal attack on a child sparks rising tensions, putting Pete in the crosshairs of a town on the brink of violence.

With outlaws, corrupt landowners, and a town full of secrets standing in his way, Pete races against time to expose the truth, protect the innocent, and stop the sheriff's tragic fate. But some people will do anything to keep the past buried—including burying Pete alive. Can Pete outsmart history again, or will this trip to the Wild West be his last?

Perfect for fans of YA Westerns and time-travel adventures, The Abilene Kid: Boot Hill Curse delivers high-stakes action, historical intrigue, and a hero who refuses to let the past win.

AVAILABLE MAY 2025

ABOUT THE AUTHOR

John Madormo, Chicago area author/screenwriter has created a body of work that has attracted the attention of publishers and motion picture producers. John has signed multiple publishing contracts and has sold a family comedy screenplay to a Los Angeles production company. He is the author of over ten middle-grade and young-adult novels.